DARK MEMORY....

From the moment she saw the big middle-aged man, with his handsome, debauched face and his lazy, insulting manner, she knew there was something about him she should remember . . . something elusive . . . something troubling . . . something just out of reach . . .

Now she was certain. She would have to discover it—whatever the cost. Even if it meant returning to a past she hated. Even if it meant facing a truth she dreaded. For now it was a matter of life and death—her own . . .

"Leslie Ford continues to keep her rating up with the best in mystery makers"

—Atlanta Journal

ABOUT THE AUTHOR

LESLIE FORD has become one of the most widely read mystery writers in America. Her first novel was published in 1928 and since then she has written some forty others.

Miss Ford lives in Annapolis, Maryland.

Among her books are *False To Any Man, Old Lover's Ghost, The Town Cried Murder, The Woman in Black, Trial By Ambush, Ill Met By Moonlight, The Simple Way of Poison, The Clue of the Judas Tree, Three Bright Pebbles* and *Washington Whispers Murder*, all published in Popular Library editions.

THE BAHAMAS MURDER CASE

By LESLIE FORD

WILDSIDE PRESS

Murder in the Bahamas

Published by Wildside Press LLC
www.wildsidepress.com

Dedication:
TO KATE M. MYERS

1

Mr. Jacob Steinberg, of Miles, Case and Steinberg, attorneys-at-law, read through the letter the typist from the firm's secretarial pool brought in to him, and took up his pen.

"Thank you, that is all."

He waited till she reached the door. "Miss Davis . . . Let me emphasize what I said before. Communications from this office to a client are strictly confidential—even when they seem to be of a nature to give concern to an employee of this office. Much as we might personally like to put Miss Dayton . . . shall we say, on her guard . . . by letting her know that inquiries have been made about her, it would be a serious breach of professional ethics for any member of the firm to do so."

He tilted the envelope toward him. "Miss Dayton planned to spend her vacation in Nassau, as the guest of Scott Beckwith, our present client Mr. Charles Cavanaugh's nephew, at Mr. Cavanaugh's winter residence there? Is this the address she left for the office files?"

"Yes, sir. Except that she has it 'care of Mr. John Scott Beckwith,' Scott Beckwith's father. Not his uncle Mr. Cavanaugh. Betsy—I mean Miss Dayton—thought it was the Beckwiths' house. She never mentioned him." Miss Davis nodded toward the envelope addressed to Mr. Charles Cavanaugh. "Not when she talked to me anyway."

"That's all then, Miss Davis."

He waited again until the girl had gone, the impressive if slightly pompous courtroom pursing of his jowls and lips relaxing as he continued to watch her in his mind for an instant. He hoped he had been impressive and pompous enough for Miss Davis to understand him completely, in a difficult and certainly unusual matter. He knew she was bright, and she had looked sufficiently bewildered to convince him that if she had not understood him, she would when she thought it over. He picked up the letter and the inquiry from Mr. Charles Cavanaugh that it was in answer to, and crossed the office to his library and conference room. Sandwiches, milk, and coffee were at two places at the oak table in the center of the room. Jacob Steinberg glanced at his watch, waiting for the senior member of the firm.

"Thank you for coming, sir," he said. He closed the door behind the wizened, silver-haired realist who specialized in contracts and who thought Jacob Steinberg their trial lawyer an able but hopeless romantic.

He waited for Judge Miles to take his place at the head of the table. "Do you remember, sir," he asked then, "eleven years ago, when you told me to pull in my horns, and bet me——"

"Vaguely," Judge Miles said. Steinberg smiled as he saw him reach for the pocket he kept his billfold in. Judge Miles was never vague about anything connected with law or money. "Dayton Associates," Judge Miles said. He thought for an instant. "Jerome Dayton put through a deal to build and operate a chemical plant in the Argentine. He collected just under two hundred thousand dollars from friends, in cash. He decided to abscond—with his secretary. Miss . . . Gurney. Miss Ethel Gurney. He committed suicide when his warehouse caught fire with the secretary and the money trapped inside."

"Or so the New York police held."

"And which you objected to," Judge Miles continued dryly, "with no standing in the case and no admissible evidence. Your theory, I seem to recall, being based on the presumed facts that Jerome Dayton was not the kind of man to abscond with his friends' money, and that Miss Gurney was neither so attractive nor so stupid. Let me see . . . she had phoned you here, that morning, making an urgent appointment for the following day. Presumably she would not have done so if she had been planning on immediate flight with Jerome Dayton and the money."

"Jerome Dayton," Steinberg said gravely, "was known to have a heart condition. It was a normal act on his part—under the shock of arriving at the warehouse to find Miss Gurney burned to death and the money destroyed by the flames—for him to take one of the pills he carried, with no intention of taking his life."

"The pill he took being cyanide . . . Dayton's business being chemicals." Judge Miles shook his head. "He had no
6

known enemies. He had with him a full bottle of his proper pills, in addition to the empty bottle the cyanide tablet presumably came out of. His prescription had been refilled that morning."

"Do you recall who picked up the prescription, that morning, at the pharmacist's?"

"His secretary, Ethel Gurney, I presume."

"So the police did, until it was established that she never got farther uptown than Fourteenth Street that day. The pharmacy was in the East Sixties. They began looking then for the other young woman who had worked in Dayton's office, and who apparently had picked the prescription up, shortly before twelve o'clock. She was Miss Gurney's assistant. But by the time they got around to looking for her, she had calmly walked out of the small apartment she lived in, near Miss Gurney's, and simply disappeared. Ethel Gurney had been fond enough of her to leave her two hundred dollars in her will, along with a pathetic little diamond crescent watch pin that had belonged to Gurney's mother, and the muskrat coat she'd bought with her Christmas bonus. None of which did this woman come forward to collect . . . and she has never been heard of since."

Jacob Steinberg looked down at the letters in his hand.

"That is why I am greatly interested in anyone who is still interested in any of the Daytons," he said quietly. "Where does such a woman go? If she got another job, she could be found through her social security number, but she never has. How does any normal, efficient young woman manage to be so self-effacing that nobody, at the time of the Dayton catastrophe, so much as thought of her, until Ethel Gurney's will turned up? Her landlady did not know she was gone until the rent was overdue. That young woman has always fascinated me, Judge. I thought for a while I had sold myself—and her—to the police. And in fact I had . . . until they turned up the two second-hand bags at the airport, checked under assumed names, with Dayton's and Ethel Gurney's clothes in them. They had nearly lost interest when the autopsy showed Dayton's death was due to cyanide, clearly self-administered—the taxi driver saw him swallow the tablet when he got to the burning plant. The suitcases were all the police needed. What difference did it make that the other woman had disappeared? Why should she come back to a job that was no longer there? Who cared what had happened to her? Poor Ethel Gurney was burned to death in the warehouse fire, Dayton had committed suicide, and that was that. C'est la vie."

"It seemed to me they lost interest quite reasonably," Judge Miles said. "That was when I advised you to pull in your horns—and why I bet you a hundred dollars against ten, which was all you could afford at the time, that we would never hear of the matter again." He opened his billfold. "I take it I've lost the hundred?"

Steinberg shook his head, smiling. "It's not the bet, Judge. It's the horns. You didn't advise me to pull them in—you told me to. Well, they're out again now."

He handed the two letters over, waiting while the senior partner read through them.

Judge Miles gave them back and took off his spectacles. "Your horns were out again when you hired Elizabeth Dayton, last summer while I was away," he said dryly. "I saw her personal file and noted she was Jerome Dayton's daughter. Did you also arrange for her to meet Scott Beckwith, whose uncle Mr. Charles Cavanaugh is for some reason so concerned as to inquire of us why she is coming to Nassau, and what she may have found out in this office about her father's death?"

Steinberg shook his head again. "You make me more Machiavellian than I am, Judge. Elizabeth Dayton applied for a job here. I didn't go out and bring her in. Young Beckwith met her here, but that was his own idea, not mine. I didn't know Scott Beckwith was Mr. Charles Cavanaugh's nephew, for the simple reason that I did not and do not know Mr. Charles Cavanaugh, and never heard of him until I got the letter you have just read, in which he asks us for that information about Miss Dayton. For the same reason, I don't know why Mr. Cavanaugh is so concerned. That's why I'm sticking my horns out again, Judge. I believe in Chance. I see it work too often not to believe in it. I don't know why Miss Dayton happened to choose us. She needed a job, we had one. I don't know why Scott Beckwith invited her to Nassau, except that she's a very attractive girl. I don't know why his uncle Charles Cavanaugh should burst in this way. There was never anyone named Cavanaugh in the Dayton case."

He tapped the letter in his hand. "But, as you can see, he has an intimate knowledge of the whole thing. I hope my reply——"

"If what you believe about the Dayton case should be

true," Judge Miles said, "I hope your reply will protect her. She could be in danger."

He got to his feet and went to the windows, moving aside the long curtains. The wind was driving the smoke-dyed sleet in angry splinters across the bleak canyon before him. The thermometer facing the window stood at twenty-two. Below him in the street the noon-hour crowds swarmed along, bent forward, like a host of trundling beetles too confused to hunt for cover.

"It must be lovely in Nassau right now. I have always liked the Bahama Islands. I hope Miss Dayton has learned that sharks infest the pleasantest waters."

He crossed the room to the door. "Thank you for lunch, Jacob. I've heard they sometimes tether lambs out to attract wolves . . . or is it tigers? I've never heard of their being used for sharks. I trust Miss Dayton is not eaten, and enjoys her holiday . . . at your expense, as I shall keep the hundred. It's a pity there is no way of letting her know that inquiries have been made."

2

The small gray lizard on the golden coconut palm by the terrace pool gave his head a tentative upward dart. The woman lying in the slanting shadows on the bamboo chaise longue, her gaze fixed rigidly on the toe of her green linen shoe, had been so still it almost seemed safe for him to move. A sharp rap-rap froze him where he was. John Scott Beckwith Sr., stopping at the top of the stone steps down from the upper garden level, was knocking his pipe out, very deliberately, because now that he had found his wife, hidden from view of the house by the massive bank of salmon-pink bougainvillea, any small delaying tactic was acceptable to him. He reminded himself that he was from Boston and an essentially reasonable and patient man. Twenty-eight years of a semi-neutral buffer state between the never patient and rarely reasonable individuals and factions of the tribe of Cavanaughs—his wife's tribe—had left him only slightly weary, though at the moment damned well irritated with the whole lot of them. Except his wife. He was still quietly but profoundly in love with her. Otherwise he would not have felt the need of knocking his pipe out for so long, to delay having to go down and make himself sound patient and reasonable when what he wanted to do was take her abominable brother by the scruff of the neck and throw him out of the house.

Certain things were opposed to such an act, however, John Beckwith reflected. For one thing, the house belonged to her brother. For another, John Beckwith had never in his life done anything more violent than sit at a desk as president of a conservative banking institution. Also, unfortunately, Charles Cavanaugh had been an athlete and a first-rate boxer in his youth, and he was still a powerful man in spite of everything he had done to wreck himself. Besides that, you couldn't help like the poor devil, no matter what he did. Always, right after you'd decided now you were really through, this time he had to get out and stay out, something happened—his Irish charm, his sudden overwhelming generosities, even a kindly worldly wisdom he had, made you go on putting up with him. And that's the way it would be until somebody knocked him over the head some night, John Scott Beckwith reflected, and then Charles Cavanaugh would become a legend. Everybody would forget what an unbearable stinker he'd been, half if not three-fourths of the time. Just as John Scott Beckwith would have to watch himself now. Let him say one word about Charles Cavanaugh, even tacitly agree with what his wife herself had said, much less repeat it after her, and she'd be up in arms. "You can't say things like that about my brother! You just don't understand him!" It had happened before, and it would happen again.

He gave his pipe a final tap on the stone lichen-stained balustrade and went on down. He hoped she wouldn't be crying. She cried so seldom that to see her finally beaten down to tears was harrowing. But she wasn't. As he came around the rim of the pool she moved brimstone blue eyes slowly from the toe of her shoe and looked up at him, and moved them back. John Beckwith glanced up behind him at the house. He had left his brother-in-law up there, in the living room, a gin-and-tonic in his hand, his chin on his collar, staring at the grass rug, still dressed in the tweed jacket and flannel trousers he'd worn down from Long Island —whether himself, or not himself, as his sister euphemistically put it, John Beckwith could not say. It had got so it was hard to tell.

He looked hopefully at the stone steps. He didn't want Charles Cavanaugh to break his neck, but if he broke a leg or something, they could put him in a plane and ship him over to Miami to a hospital for the next two weeks. He knew it was a vain hope. Charles Cavanaugh was indestructible. He had broken everything you could name, from the law to the cover of the tank of the water closet, but he had never broken any piece or portion of Charles Cavanaugh. The problem now was only what to say to Charles Cavanaugh's younger sister that would not, John Beckwith thought with a kind of wry humor, channel the storm his way and leave her brother to ride the calm and open sea that would follow it. Experience told him there was nothing. He sat down in the white iron chair beside her, took his pouch out of his pocket and began methodically to fill his pipe, waiting.

Then he looked at her with a sudden new anxiety. There

was something wrong with the scene they had played for so many years he would have thought he could read her lines as well as he could his own. The slow-burning anger quickened inside him. He put it down savagely, aware that it was only a part, though a dangerous part, of the maddening futility of the whole thing. He waited a little until he could speak without his voice betraying him.

"This won't help, Nell," he said. "I know it's damnable, to have it happen now of all times. But don't take it this way, old girl."

Eleanor Beckwith drew her breath in slowly and held it a long quivering moment before she let it go again.

"I don't know what way I am taking it," she said quietly. "I don't know whether I'm sickest, or maddest." Her quick, mobile face looked each in turn. "It makes me so sick I could die and so mad I could go up there and kill him with my own hands. The first time our son has ever faintly indicated he was seriously interested in a girl he was bringing to see us, this has to happen. Just when we'd like to appear as a respectable, pleasant family, his wretched uncle has to come and spoil it all. It makes me furious. I could kill him. It makes me so sick I want to crawl off under a bush and simply die."

"For the love of heaven, Nell . . ." John Beckwith spoke with a kind of helpless desperation. "It's not that bad. It would have been pleasanter, certainly. But Scott's been around his uncle a long time. If this Betsy girl works in a law office, she's presumably been exposed to . . . to some of the evils of the outside world. We don't *know* the boy wants to marry her, but if so, and she cares a rap about him, she's hardly likely to walk out on him because his Uncle Charles is a———"

He stopped, expecting her to flash hotly around, daring him to say the word. "You can't *talk* that way about my brother!" It had happened so often for so long that he was not quite sure what word he would have used if he had ever been allowed to get far enough to use it. It would have been hard to pick any single right word. The earlier phases of Charles Cavanaugh's career had at least had a kind of flamboyant lustiness. He had been a devil, but a gay, openhearted, openhanded devil you wanted to throttle but never disown. He had thrown money right and left, but he had an extraordinary talent for making it; he played around with women, but they were always, so far as his family knew, women who were old enough and experienced enough to

12

look after themselves if they wanted to. He drank too much, but he could always stop.

Until just before the war, when he had gradually stopped doing anything else. Then the war had snapped him out of that, and only John Beckwith had had the uneasy and strange feeling that his half-dozen citations for valor beyond the call of duty were really for something very different and very curious. Charles Cavanaugh had seemed to him consciously determined never to come back alive. He had asked him about it once, only half jokingly, and Charles Cavanaugh had looked at him solemnly, got up without a word and gone out to help his sister mix a cocktail at the bar. At the end of the war he had come back to the Beckwiths, without so much as a superficial scratch in spite of everything, and within a month he was on the old routine. Seeming to need them, and living with them, he still lived off in a detached and solitary world of his own, every day more moody and more unpredictable. And several times recently . . . John Beckwith shut the door of his mind abruptly. If he ever consciously admitted the vague apprehensions that had stirred in it the last month or so, he would have to take some sort of active step that he knew would be fatal to his own happiness. Looking at his wife now, he felt as he had felt before, like a man turning his back on a faint plume of smoke at the end of the wheat because he was afraid of trampling down the ripe grain if he went to put the fire out.

"We'll just have to make the best of it, Nell," he said. It was grossly inadequate, but it was all he could think of. "We've done it before."

"I know. But this is different. Something's got into Charles. And don't tell me I'm being fanciful—I can't bear it. I've thought this before, at home. When Scott wanted to bring Betsy Dayton there before we came down here, and I told Charles, that was the week he *really* went off. That's when I called Scott and told him how much nicer I thought it would be if he'd wait and bring her down here." She turned her head not to have to look at him. "Then when Charles . . . came to, I asked him. He said he'd never heard of anyone named Dayton, so I forgot about it. Now I wish I'd kept at him. He can't know her—not if she's a nice girl. But there's *something*. Otherwise why has he come down here now?"

John Beckwith shrugged. "It's his house, my dear."

"It's been his house for five years and he's never been in it since the week end he bought it. I'll bet he hadn't the faintest idea what he was doing when he did it. I've asked him down every winter and he says he hates sun and sand and the devil couldn't find him dead in Nassau. He's just here to make trouble, John, and he's——"

At the sharp crashing sound from the upper terrace she flashed around, the back of her clenched fist pressed to her mouth. John Scott Beckwith was half-way up the steps when he heard a second duller crash. From the upper level a half-dozen oranges and grapefruit came bouncing down between his feet.

"John—come back! Please!"

He looked down at his wife and went on up the steps. Charles Cavanaugh was still there where he had left him. It was not Charles Cavanaugh who had crashed into the fruit trees, and if he had heard it at all it had not disturbed him. He was sitting there, a serene and almost childlike smile on his face.

John Beckwith had started across the terrace when he heard his wife call again. He turned to go down to her and stopped, stiffening a little as he saw what it was. The woman next door was smiling at him, through the opening in the stone wall that until a moment ago had been firmly closed up with the section of pink, painted boards now lying between the orange and grapefruit trees planted to conceal it. Mrs. Huse-Lorne's glossy, golden hair glistened in the sunlight. Her white teeth glistened between her scarlet lips, curved in a dimpling provocative smile that at the same time conveyed a mocking and malicious triumph. Three native workmen were picking up the boards. Mrs. Huse-Lorne's slender hand with long, scarlet nails was resting lightly on the wrought-iron gate that the pink boards had immobilized for the five years the Beckwiths had been her neighbors. She was still smiling. John Beckwith, feeling like an awkward fool, stood staring at her.

"At long last we're going to be really friends and neighbors, Mr. Beckwith." She laughed. "We're charmed, really. But this gate does want oiling, I'm afraid. Perhaps your man will attend to it? And do tell Mrs. Beckwith how really pleased we are to help. We'll see you all later." She smiled again and turned to her workmen. "You boys get this brushed up, and blacken both sides of the gate. The bars are rusty on the Beckwith side."

As she moved off she brushed the rust from the Beckwith side gracefully from her fingertips. John Beckwith still stood

14

there, completely blank except for an acute awareness that for the shy and retiring widow with the soft, southern accent who had crept into Nassau the year before the war when the Beckwiths still had the big house on Hog Island, Mrs. Huse-Lorne was a transformation that was little short of miraculous—down to and including the accent she must have picked up from the Major Huse-Lorne she had married the third year she was there. He went over to the steps and down toward his wife. The open gate in the wall was really staggering. The pink painted boards that had blocked it up the past five years had been more than pink boards closing a gate in a nine-foot stone wall. They had been a symbol of one woman's violent and, it seemed to John Beckwith, being married to her, almost maniacally irrational antipathy to another that he had long given up even remotely trying to understand. And now the blockade was lifted, they were going to be friends and neighbors, the Huse-Lornes would be seeing them all later. So intent was he on trying to recall some wisp of straw in the domestic wind that should have prepared him for this extraordinary reversal that he did not realize he was smiling until Eleanor Beckwith flared out at him. Her face was flushed, blistering, angry tears wetting her dark lashes.

"Stop grinning like an ape! I *had* to do it! She got me where I couldn't do anything else and not look like a snobbish boor! So quit being so damned male and superior about everything!"

"What—"

"If you'll hush for a minute and quit interrupting me every time I open my mouth I'll tell you," she said hotly. "I was talking about it to some of my friends at the Red Cross this morning. I didn't even know the woman was in the room. I said my son was bringing his girl over and I didn't know where I was going to put her." Her eyes flashed blue fire. "And don't look as if you thought I'd lost my mind! Where would *you* put her? We've only got three bedrooms and two baths. I can't send Charles to a hotel—I wouldn't have a moment's peace in the first place, and it's his house. I can't send Scott out and give the child his room and have to tell her to use our bath and keep her doors locked because Scott's uncle has lost his sense of direction and wanders around half the night. What else could I do? You never stop to think of the *mechanics* of having a guest in the house!"

15

John Beckwith frowned. "No, I'm afraid I don't," he said contritely.

"We've put up other people's guests often enough. And before anybody could breathe, she burst in. 'My deah Mrs. Beckwith.'" Her voice took on Andrea Huse-Lorne's high glittering accent. "'You realleh must use our guest cottage. We'd adore for you to use it, my deah. We realleh would. It's just a step through the wicket.' And then, before I could say Thanks very much but we'd manage, she said, 'And if you'd be kind enough to use the cottage, Mrs. Beckwith, then I wouldn't be embarrassed at asking you if we might use your garden for the overflow meeting of my Girl Guides when you're away. The sweet things, they do so appreciate the kindness of the American winter people . . .'"

Eleanor Beckwith put her hands out. "What could I do? After all the fuss I'd made about needing a place, I either had to accept the one right next door or sound like an ungrateful, stiff-necked snob.—And of course I'm delighted to have the cottage. It gets Betsy out of the house away from my wretched brother, and still close enough so she's practically in it, and that nice maid of theirs sleeps in the room just below so she's not alone. But I still don't trust that woman, and I *hate* Charles for putting me in a position . . . Well, let's go up. You meet the kids and I'll stay and keep my eye on Charles. I don't want him roaming around Nassau before they get here."

She started towards the steps, turned, caught her husband's arm and dropped her head impulsively against his shoulder. "Oh, John—this is going to be a nightmare! I do so hope she's all right, but no matter what she is, if Scott does want to marry her, we're not going to *let* Charles break it up!— And if I only hadn't had to knuckle down to That Woman Next Door! I know it's going to mean trouble. She's just the kind of woman Charles is likely to go all out for. I *know* there's going to be trouble!"

John Beckwith tightened his arm around her. None of the domestic platitudes seemed to fit. He was not an imaginative man, but he had somewhere a sharply disturbed feeling of mischief impending, a chilling sense that something damned unpleasant could be brewing. He shook his head impatiently as he patted his wife's shoulder.

"Don't worry. We——"

She raised her head quickly, listening. "John!" She

16

clutched his arm. "John, they've come—that's Scott. Hurry, John! They must have caught the earlier plane."

He heard his son's voice then as she ran ahead of him up the steps. "Hey? Anybody home?" And then his, "Hi, Ma, there you are! This is Betsy, Mother. Where's Dad?"

A sudden chill that was not of anything impending but practical and immediate came to John Beckwith. The "Anybody home?" could only mean they hadn't seen Charles Cavanaugh sitting there in the living room . . . and if Charles had moved out onto the town, Betsy Dayton's introduction to the Beckwiths could easily be something. He took his handkerchief out of his pocket and wiped his moist forehead.

"Damn him!" he whispered fervently. He stiffened his shoulders and went on up to meet the girl whose coming seemed somehow to be the focal point of a gathering storm. "A cloud no bigger than a man's hand," he thought wryly.

Then, at the top of the steps, his mind cleared and the lines between his gray brows relaxed. It was like coming up out of a haunted cellar into the broad, clean-smelling sunlight. He could see her standing there beside Scott, the top of her head reaching just above his shoulder, taller than Eleanor, slender and straight as a young palm, with soft, brown, curly hair, with golden highlights glistening in the sun, something so fresh and clear and wonderfully normal and simple about her that he was really aware for the first time how profoundly anxious he had been.

3

He quickened his step across the garden. He had not, he was reflecting, really given his son credit for this much good taste or good sense. He hoped his wife's motherly intuitions were right for once and Scott was at last seriously interested. Betsy Dayton had dancing brown eyes, a wide, red mouth and a firm, solid chin. He found himself taking an almost professional inventory, as if she were an applicant for a job in the public relations end of the bank, and his respect for his son reached an unexpected high. This was the kind of girl they'd really like to have around.

Scott Beckwith gripped his hand. "Hi, Dad! I want you to meet Betsy Dayton."

Proud as a young peacock, John Beckwith thought. *Maybe Nell's right.* Suddenly remembering, he shot a swift glance into the house at the empty chair where Charles Cavanaugh had been, and caught the sharp questioning anxiety in his wife's eyes meeting his. He put his hand out to Betsy Dayton. Pride in his girl, in himself and in his family was something John Beckwith wanted his six-foot-two son to keep as long as he could. He remembered his pride in his own parents, and the agonizing embarrassment at a fey cousin of his mother's who did nothing more harmful than gather table scrap to feed the pigeons in Harvard Yard.

"Welcome, Betsy!" he heard himself saying cordially. He shook the girl's firm slender hand. "It's good to have you here."

"It's wonderful to be here," Betsy Dayton said. "Oh, it really *is* beautiful, isn't it? I've never been in the Bahamas, and I never believed it was actually like the pictures."

She was thinking: *I wonder what's the matter? Something's wrong. Why do they keep looking inside? Maybe we shouldn't have taken the early plane. Or is it me, some way? Maybe they're afraid I'm going to marry their son.*

She looked past his father's graying head at Scott Beckwith. He was much more like his mother, except for his reddish sandy hair and his straight firm mouth. Maybe it had been a mistake for her to come at all, except that his mother's letter had sounded so cordial she'd thought they really meant they liked Scott to bring his friends. And the chance of two weeks in the sun, if she took her vacation in the winter, and of an unexpected bonus, thanks to Mr. Steinberg, to pay expenses, were more than she'd been able to resist. But parents of sons were funny people, especially when they had a lot of money, and obviously the Beckwiths had. All you had to do was look at them and look at the house. Somehow it hadn't occurred to her, the way Scott talked. And they were certainly jittery about something.

She smiled at Mr. Beckwith. "I'm afraid barging in early like this must be an awful nuisance. But we got to Miami earlier than we thought, and Scott——"

"It's not that, Betsy," Scott said. He pulled a chair out into the sun, took off his coat and rolled up his sleeves. "Boy, this is wonderful! Why don't we all relax—especially you, Mother? We saw him just now in Bay Street. And Betsy's a big girl now, so we can tell her all."

His frosty blue eyes crinkled with amusement as he turned from his mother to Betsy Dayton. "It's my Uncle Charles. He's a fugitive from Alcoholics Anonymous. A wonderful guy, but a pain in the neck to have around." He grinned at Betsy. "We have him around because Mother's an old softie, and anyway he's stinking rich and if we kicked him out some dame would get him."

"Oh, *Scott!*"

Betsy saw Mrs. Beckwith's blue eyes kindle and the sparks begin to fly. Nevertheless she was aware that the tension in both the Beckwiths had relaxed with a kind of sudden magic. *How miserable for them,* she thought. But the big man Scott had pointed out a few minutes ago in Bay Street, riding in a native carriage with a sharp-beaked little man in a dirty yachting cap, hadn't seemed so appallingly disreputable. In fact he looked more like Scott than Scott's father did, and very attractive in a heavy-set sophisticated sort of way. He had passed them before Scott could be sure he'd recognized him, not expecting him to be in Nassau, but she remembered now there was something like a slight groan when he'd said, "I'm very much afraid that was Uncle Charles in person."

"My son's just being objectionable, Betsy," Mrs. Beckwith said. "Pay no——"

"Come, come, Mother." Scott grinned over at his father. "Let's not tell Betsy any fibs she can catch us out on later. She's a very smart girl. Think of the years you've been saying thank heaven Uncle Charles didn't come down here, with that Jezebel living next door."

He clasped his hands behind his head and raised it to look over the pink-washed wall that divided their small elegantly simple house from Mrs. Huse-Lorne's large and luxuriously elaborate one. "How is Jezebel, by the way? By that I mean, how are Relations? More strained, less strained, or just the same strain as always?"

Betsy saw the bright flush that burned for an instant in Mrs. Beckwith's tanned cheeks before she turned and busied herself brushing the ants off the great salmon-yellow hibiscus blossoms growing against the pillars of the open gallery. Mr. Beckwith had leaned over to knock his pipe out against a tub of gardenias. *Tactless*, she thought. That it was not being taken the way Scott had intended and expected was quite apparent.

"Relations with the Huse-Lornes couldn't be pleasanter," Mrs. Beckwith said calmly. "In fact, Mrs. Huse-Lorne has very kindly allowed us to use her guest cottage for Betsy while you're both here." The flush was gone from her cheeks. She smiled pleasantly. "My brother's arrival sort of put us on a spot. There are only three bedrooms in the house, so I was delighted when Mrs. Huse-Lorne suggested we use her cottage."

She moved toward the living room. "I'll just go phone and tell her you've come. You probably would like to change and get a little sun before lunch. You can be as naked as you like out here in the garden. Scott's probably told you the Nassauvians hate Americans who go around in shorts and bra tops in the public streets. Not that you would, of course."

She's not sure what I would do, Betsy Dayton thought. Still, she was nice—attractive and young-looking. *If she'd just relax again.* First it had been Uncle Charles, and now it was apparently Mrs. Huse-Lorne, tying her up in a tight sort of brittle knot.

Betsy smiled at Mr. Beckwith and his son. "This is *wonderful*," she said happily. "It's been so rainy and cold at home." She was really saying to both of them, "Don't . . . Let's not bother about Uncle Charles and Mrs. Huse-Lorne. It's too exciting and lovely here to worry about other people's problems."

20

A small, gray lizard scurried across the terrace. A mockingbird was trilling in the salmon bougainvillea, a hummingbird darted and hovered and darted on again among the myriad tiny coral trumpets of a feathery bush in the white sunlight against the wall at the end of the terrace. Scott Beckwith opened his eyes and put his hand out, lightly touching her slender foot. "—happy?"

Betsy Dayton nodded. It was utter and enchanted peace. After six months as the youngest secretary in the law offices of Miles, Case and Steinberg, she had almost forgotten there was anything left but pushing and clamoring, intrigue and chicanery, despair and bitterness. For two weeks she could forget it, and it was going to be wonderful to be off in a small cottage by herself. She turned her head and looked across the terrace. She could see one rose-pink corner of it through the iron gate. The gleaming slate of its tiny hipped roof showed above the paler pink of the flower-decked wall behind the citrus trees, their golden fruit hanging like jewels among the dark shining leaves. To be there, with solitude and privacy, after the small dank apartment where she and her mother were always tangled up in each other's slips and stockings drying in the single bathroom, was going to be sheer heaven. For that matter, it was probably a relief to Scott and his family. After all, he hadn't known her but a couple of months, and he'd been sweet, asking her down. She hadn't known till then that he had a family, or that they had a house in Nassau, or anything about him, except that he was a cut above most of the firm's clients who invited the secretaries out to lunch. Not that Scott was a client. He was just from a bank trying to unravel a customer who was their client.

She looked down at him, warmly aware of his fingertips still resting on the toe of her shoe, and surprised at herself for feeling that way about it . . . *You'd better be careful, Betsy. He's just being kind to a working girl.* Falling in love with him would mess everything up—for her at least . . . *Watch yourself, Betsy—no going home with a sun-tanned hide and a blistered heart.*

She glanced around toward the living room, aware that Mr. Beckwith had got quickly to his feet at the silvery peal of a bell.

"I expect it's Charles."

Scott raised his head and opened his eyes. "Good." He spoke with no enthusiasm. "Cross your fingers," he murmured to Betsy. "With Uncle Charles, one never knows. You're going to like the Huse-Lorne's cottage," he added. "It's quiet. Huse-Lorne won't know you're there as soon as she finds out you work for a living."

He spoke lightly, but she saw he was listening intently toward the inside of the house.

I am certainly going to like the Huse-Lornes' cottage, Betsy Dayton thought.

4

Andrea Huse-Lorne turned, brushing the smudge of rusted iron from the gate off her fingertips with a pleasure as triumphant as she had ever hoped to feel. It had taken real effort to smile charmingly, not to laugh aloud, in Mr. John Scott Beckwith's superior and stupefied face as he stood there, staring like a dazed idiot at the pink boards lying on the ground, before he trotted back to his wife to find out what was going on. Of course she wouldn't have told him, not before she had to. The blank stupidity on Mr. Beckwith's face was only slightly less pleasurable than the astonished dismay on Madam's, earlier that day, when she had had to accept the gracious offer of the cottage. Andrea Huse-Lorne restrained herself, moving across her garden, until she sank down in the canopied lounge seat beside her terrace swimming pool. Then she laughed, long and with genuine delight. To bring Mrs. John Beckwith to heel was the crowning touch of a day that was already one of signal trimph in her carefully planned career in the capital of the Bahama Islands. Having chosen a small exclusive world, for a very deliberate purpose and a vitally important reason, Mrs. Huse-Lorne had made it her oyster. The two pearls she had picked out of it that morning were two of the best. Her appointment as Honorary President of the Annual Gymkhana might mean nothing in terms of world supremacy, but to Mrs. Huse-Lorne in Nassau it meant a great deal. Bringing Mrs. Beckwith to heel was barely second. Only two things were left for her to achieve before she could rest, take off the elephant hide she had developed, and start giving back some of the poisoned barbs she had taken. The Beckwiths were one step in the direction of the first of them: the exclusive club of her own countrymen on Hog Island. The other would have to wait until the providential death of her husband's superannuated male relative. As Lady Huse-Lorne she might even move to Washington and take over there. She could . . . if she decided she wanted to.

The laughter went slowly out of her face as she looked over at the small pink cottage that had been the honey in the trap for Eleanor Beckwith. What to do with them, now she had them? With Scott Beckwith's girl as her resident guest there, they couldn't refuse a cocktail party for her. Or a small dinner. She could have more people at cocktails, but twenty-four at a dinner would underline her new relationship much more skilfully. She began going over in her head a list of Americans who could not refuse an invitation to dinner in honor of the girl Scott Beckwith must be planning to marry, from the coy and proprietary way his mother had acted that morning. And time would be of the essence; she had to get in before they were dated up. Andrea Huse-Lorne got to her feet. Wednesday the Acting Governor and his black-haired, pink-cheeked wife were dining with her anyway, to go over plans for the Annual Gymkhana. She crossed the terrace into the cool shadowed depths of her slate-blue and dull-gold drawing room, its color shrewdly planned to deepen the blue of her slanting eyes and highlight the gleaming gold of her sleekly-groomed hair. She sat down at the Queen Anne desk at the end of the room, took the pad and the gold pencil there and began making her list.

> The Acting Governor and Mrs. Mayfield
> Mr. and Mrs. John Scott Beckwith Sr.
> Mr. Charles Cavanaugh

Mrs. Huse-Lorne hesitated. She had never met Mr. Charles Cavanaugh, but she had seen him arrive that morning. Attractive, and unattached, she knew from the agent who had sold him the house. Furthermore, if it hadn't been for his coming down, none of this would ever have happened. She put a double star by Charles Cavanaugh's name. She then smiled happily, made another double star for the next entry, and wrote after it,

> Girl

In her excitement in seeing and grabbing the opportunity tossed in her lap, she had neither heard nor cared what the girl's name was.

She finished her list and surveyed it, reached for the phone and stopped as she heard the door upstairs on the street level of the house open and the rattle of her husband's golf clubs as he stowed them in the hall closet. She straightened her face out abruptly. Ramsay Huse-Lorne had developed an unexpected recalcitrant and stubborn attitude toward her siege of the Beckwiths. She waited, hand on the phone, to see if he would come straight down or go on into his bedroom upstairs. Her eyes brightened as she listened to his lumbering step overhead.

As she turned to the phone again it rang.

"Mrs. Huse-Lorne hyeah."

Then she relaxed, smiling at herself in the mirrored panel by the door to the hall.

"Oh, Mrs. Beckwith . . . how sweet of you to call . . . My deah, of course! Just take the child right over—the cottage is all ready. I'll send a maid along immediately. I'm sure everything's in order. There's even a key if she wishes to lock the door at night, although of course we never do . . ."

She drew the dinner list toward her, still smiling.

"And my dear, I do want to have three or four people in to a small sort of family dinner, Wednesday night . . . That's the only evening the Acting Governor and his wife have free for some time . . ."

When Mrs. Huse-Lorne put the phone down she brushed her fingers off lightly a second time, and straightened her face out a second time. Her husband was coming down the curving outside stairs from the balcony overhead. She turned and saw him pause at the bottom, craning his neck inside to see if she was there. He was in his bathing trunks, with a towel over his arm. There was an open letter in his hand. A begging letter from some of his moldy, moth-eaten relatives in England, Andrea Huse-Lorne thought, lifting her brows. She regarded him with sudden distaste. Long and lanky, with a colorless mustache that drooped the way the rest of him drooped, including the absurd, black bathing drawers that came almost to his knobby, hairy knees, he looked like a worn-out cow with inverted straw for horns. The image of Charles Cavanaugh flashed unaccountably through her mind, brightening it for an instant as she contrasted it with the hollow-chested vacuity of the man she had married.

She smiled pleasantly at him.

"Oh, darling . . . The most extraordinary thing has happened. Two of them, in fact. Do come in—you're dry, you won't hurt the rug."

His refusal to come into the drawing room in his swimming clothes managed to irritate her increasingly, as so many of his ridiculous formalities had begun to do since she had less and less need of them and of him to get her where she wanted to go. But she was too pleased with herself this morning to mind. She shook out the folds of her white-linen skirt with a casual gesture, to conceal the inner pleasure that not even his eccentricities could dampen at the moment.

"It's a bore, I suppose, but they've asked me to be head of the Gymkhana next year," she said easily. "And I suppose I *ought* to do it, really. Anyway, I've accepted. And the other thing's amazing to say the least."

She let him stand moon-faced on the threshold while she tapped the desk thoughtfully with the gold pencil. "The gate to the Beckwiths through the wall is opened, and young Scott Beckwith's fiancée is going to occupy our guest cottage. If you can manage to believe that."

She watched his Adam's apple come up and go back down again in the elongated, sun-reddened neck. He didn't tan. He got red and peeled and got red again, no matter how long he stayed in the sub-tropics.

"She really put me on a spot," she went on calmly. "At the Red Cross this morning. What *was* she going to do with the girl? It would be perfectly ghastly to have to send her to a hotel. Her dear brother—who owns the house—had come, and if there was only some place . . . My dear, she was looking straight at me."

Huse-Lorne tugged at one end of his drooping mustache. "I see," he said. "Damned decent of you, and all that."

Why she was pretending to be so offhand about it, he couldn't imagine. She must actually be bursting with joy, at finally getting two things she'd worked for with relentless and positively offensive lack of any subtlety whatsoever. Up to now there had been a sort of crass honesty in her blatant maneuverings that was about all he found left to admire in her. It was precisely on that account that he had put off as long as he could coming home after he had gone to the post office. He shifted the letter to his other hand and swallowed uncomfortably. There was something a little horrible, as well as acutely painful, in knowing what open delight she would have at the news it contained. It would be worse if she pretended to be sorry.

"Here's a letter you might read," he said. "From my cousin. Afraid the old chap's about kaput."

He reached a bony red arm in, put the letter on a table by the door and backed off, looking the other way, not wanting to see the unholy joy in her face at the news that he was virtually in possession of the poverty-stricken title he had never wanted and that only two wars had put him anywhere near coming into. But he felt it, and he heard the sharply drawn and inexpressibly exultant breath she had not been alert enough to repress. He knew that only her extraordinary will power was keeping her there at his mother's desk instead of dashing over to snatch up the letter that meant her third triumph of the morning.

He went across the blue-tiled floor and out toward the terrace pool, looking over to see if the boarding behind the iron gate really was down. He stopped, looking myopically across the grass, and fished in his trunks pocket for his distance spectacles.

"Oh, I say," he said. His face brightened. "I say, she *is* attractive." He turned back to his wife, still at the desk, her face, bright with anticipation, fixed on the letter. "Oh, Andrea, I ran into Cavanaugh in Bay Street a bit ago. He's going to call. I must tell him to bring Miss Dayton with him. That's her name, isn't it—it was in the list of arrivals in the morning paper. Elizabeth Dayton."

He moved on out to the pool. A really attractive young woman. It was surprising, because Andrea did not normally have young and attractive women about the place. Still, the girl after all was merely a pawn in the game played over the wall.

Major Huse-Lorne did not look back at his wife again, and he did not see her sit motionless in her chair for a long instant, rigid, her hands gripping the edges of the desk, the color draining slowly out of her face. The blank stupefied disbelief in her eyes as she stared silently at him shifted then to virulent fury.

"*The fool*," Mrs. Huse-Lorne whispered. "*He's read it wrong . . .*"

But as she tried to move, to go over to the morning paper on the glass-topped table in the center of the room, a sudden crawling fear drained all the strength from her legs. She sat there helpless for an instant, and forced herself to rise then and cross the room. The flimsy newsprint ripped as her long fingernails tore it open to the list of arrivals expected in Nassau that day. Miss Elizabeth Dayton, guest of Mr. and Mrs. John Scott Beckwith Sr. and their son Mr. J. S. Beckwith Jr. Mrs. Huse-Lorne stared blindly down at the words, her hands shaking. She struggled to swallow. Her throat was parched, hard, swollen and painful. The light step of the maid coming to the door sent her into a sudden palsied frenzy that she had to fight to control.

"Shall I go help the young lady unpack, mahdam?" the girl inquired, in her soft lilting Nassauvian voice.

Andrea Huse-Lorne licked her tongue across her dry lips. "Yes." She had to tear the word from her throat. "Go quickly." She held herself rigidly erect until the girl had gone, and still holding herself erect, forced her wooden steps one after another until she had crossed the room. She went up the stairs, quickly, holding desperately to the iron railing to keep herself from breaking into open flight. Her back had been to the maid down in the drawing room. Her paralyzed brain prayed that none of the other servants would be in the hall to see her before she got to her room. Her face in the mirrored panels lighting the inside staircase was a stranger's face, ghastly and ravaged, bearing no resemblance to her own.

She made her room, locked the door behind her and ran to the door that opened into her husband's dressing room. She tore it shut and turned the key. Then she turned and stood rigidly, leaning against the door, staring desperately around her. *Not Elizabeth Dayton . . . It couldn't be . . . It was a mistake . . . a horrible, mad, insane mistake . . .* She licked her lips again and moved, as cautiously and silently as a cat, hunted or hunting, across to the window opening onto the balcony, and looked out, concealing herself behind the bougainvillea at the open louvres. Mrs. Beckwith and her son were on the porch of the tiny guest house, moving aside to let the maid in. Mrs. Huse-Lorne hardly looked at them. The triumph of seeing a Beckwith inside her grounds was dust and wormwood in her aching mouth as her drained blue eyes fastened themselves on the girl in the doorway. She was holding the door open for the maid, smiling at her and then at the two Beckwiths moving off the porch to go back through the iron gate and leave her to unpack. The white sunlight was full on her face, burnishing the soft golden tints in her brown hair.

Andrea Huse-Lorne watched her with a dull dead fascination. Suddenly she jerked her head up, sniffing the air, and started frantically back to her room. She stopped, swaying, as she clutched the side of the window and put her head against it, closing her eyes, her body shuddering in sharp convulsive waves. The odor of smoke and burning flesh was in her mind only . . . It was nowhere else, it was a hideous memory she

28

had buried and forgotten. But it was back now. The face of the girl on the porch had brought it back to haunt her with a cringing horror she had thought she never would have to fight down again. Her legs shook violently as she crept back into the room. She looked frantically around her, went over to the doors she had locked, and tried them again. Then she went, quietly and stealthily, into her own bathroom and closed the locked door.

Get rid of them. Get rid of them. The words dropped from her mind as hard and flat as the four, lethal white tablets in the sealed stoppered bottle in the small safe behind the shell-scalloped medicine cabinet over the washbowl. *Get rid of them. Get rid of them. There's nothing else to betray you.* Elizabeth Dayton had been a child then. She was in love now. She was happy. She wouldn't be thinking about the past . . . she wouldn't remember. Mrs. Huse-Lorne's hand trembled as she put it up to open the door of the cabinet. She stopped, looking across the brown reflection of her arm into her face in the mirror beyond it. She had forgotten so much that she had to remember now. She hadn't trembled then, or been afraid . . . and that time there had been nothing for her to lose. Then the four white tablets, and the fifth one, had been friends to help her, not enemies to betray. The black pupils of her eyes contracted as she turned them slowly toward the window looking down at the small, rose-pink cottage against the paler pink, flower-decked wall in the garden. She stood motionless for a moment, the breath held tightly in her lungs, her mouth hardening into a thin line.

Her hand still on the cabinet door moved, closing it quietly and deliberately. If Elizabeth Dayton did remember . . . Her hand was steady now. She straightened her shoulders, looked closely at herself in the mirror once more, turned to unlock the door of the bathroom, and stopped. She went quickly over to the dressing table and sat down on the pink-and-silver brocade seat, her hand gripping the silver handle of the mirror lying on its glass surface. She held it up, her other hand lifting the shining blonde hair that curled smoothly under her right ear in a deep, semi-pageboy bob low on the nape of her smooth, brown neck. Her hand pulled at the roots of her hair so tightly that the lines of the star-shaped scar behind her ear glistened hard and white and bloodless. She bit her lip savagely and dropped her hair back into place, her hand cupped over it as she flashed around toward the window behind her, over her dressing table.

29

Someone had passed by it, out on the balcony. A shadow had crossed the mirror she held in her hand. Her husband . . . or one of the servants? The cold snake-like dread curled and coiled around her heart. The scar . . . only her husband knew about it. And the girl. The girl who was just outside there, whom she had practically forced to be her own guest. The shadow in the mirror. The shadow of the hand of God . . . Mrs. Huse-Lorne thought suddenly. She trembled violently and put her head down on the table, her hand holding her hair cupped tightly.

5

Betsy Dayton closed the door of the cottage and stood for a moment in her miniature gallery, feeling a little like a bleached-out Northern cadaver suddenly debauched into sunlit enchantment. Total Luxury, by *Town and Country*, out of Subtropical Fairyland, she thought, with sudden amusement at the conscious perfection of every detail of the tiny establishment, even down to the gilded, specially designed key in the lock on the other side of the door.

"No dime store key this," Scott had said, picking it up when he and his mother had brought her over. He put it in the keyhole. "What's ethics about locking up and taking the key along, when you're in enemy territory, Ma?"

"Excessively bad, ethics as well as manners, I'd say—if I had any notion what you mean by 'enemy territory.'" Mrs. Beckwith had smiled, but Betsy saw the quick touch of her hand on his arm. "Let's get along and give the girl a chance to get settled and get into something cool."

She looked around her now with sheer delight. *It's so lovely.* The white, clean sunlight, the exciting smell of the salt sea in the crystal air, the clear, cloudless blue sky . . . *And I'm here.* That was the most unbelievable part of it . . . *I'm here. I'm not at the office waiting for Mr. Steinberg's buzzer to tell me some other stupid mistake I've made.* She looked across the Huse-Lornes' terraced gardens and up at the house. A tall, lanky, stoop-shouldered man in a blue-and-white striped blazer and starched white shorts was coming down the steps from the veranda. His spectacles glinted in the sun, and his pale mustache drooped as he shambled, drooping himself, across the terrace to a small white iron table set for one under an umbrella by the swimming pool. She watched him stop at the table, look at it, and turn to look up at the veranda before he sat down, unfolding his napkin across the white starched shorts.

She glanced up at the veranda. The shutters—louvres, they

were called in Bahamian houses—at the near end were partly closed. A maid with a tray was coming from the far end.

Jezebel must be busy, or indisposed, Betsy thought, as the girl stopped at a closed glass door, waited, stood there an instant and returned as she had come.

She bent down to button another six inches of the brown linen skirt she wore over her yellow shorts, and went across the terrace to the open iron gate in the wall. The short-cropped crab grass made a soundproof carpet under her feet. Short of clearing her throat or going back and slamming the gate, there was no way she could think of to warn the Beckwiths she was coming, and on the porch behind the bright screen of hibiscus they were clearly unaware of it.

"—sure Charles means it when he says he didn't mean to upset our plans." Mrs. Beckwith sounded like a woman trying to convince herself as well as her husband. "He'd just forgotten how small the house is. He's perfectly willing to go to a hotel. But . . . we don't dare let him that far out of our sight. And Betsy certainly seems like a very nice girl. I was just being silly thinking there was anything he could have against her——"

Betsy Dayton was half-way back to the gate. It was embarrassing that Mrs. Beckwith should have to reassure herself there couldn't be anything for Charles Cavanaugh to have against her—embarrassing and a little puzzling. But it didn't matter. She was too happy and too far away for any shadow of the old anxieties to reach her there. It was the Beckwiths she was thinking of and not herself when she pushed the iron gate so that it grated on the lintel to tell them she was coming. The indistinct murmur of the voices on the porch came to a stop. She went back across the grass. Mrs. Beckwith came out from behind the hibiscus as if she had never had a doubt or worry in her life.

"You do look a lot cooler, Betsy," she said smiling. "But both you and Scott are so pallid I can't bear it. I'm going to ship you both off to the Island for lunch and a swim, so run and get your suit. Scott'll be back in just a minute. He had to go down to the post office—they don't deliver mail in Nassau."

` Betsy turned back a second time. Pallid or not, it seemed pretty spur of the moment. The luncheon table on the terrace was set for five. She got her beach bag and came back again. It was spur of the moment; two plates were gone, the maid was just leaving the porch with the other mats and dishes in her hand. Uncle Charles? She thought it must be, as she felt rather than saw the muted tensing in both Beckwiths as a screen door slammed shut overhead and they waited, eyes resolutely turned away from the open stairs but all their other senses fixed on it. Apparently Scott had not been joking when he said with Uncle Charles one never knew. And they could tell without looking that he was all right. She felt them relax. They looked over then, both smiling at him as he came into sight.

It was a subtle pantomime that she would hardly have noticed if it had not been for what Scott had said. Uncle Charles seemed perfectly normal, so far as she could see, both now and in the brief moment half-an-hour before when she'd first seen him. And if he did have something against her he had managed to conceal it very well. She looked at him now with new interest. He had changed into a pair of cinnamon-colored slacks and a short-sleeved, white, knit top with faded brown stripes that made him look rather like some giant's amiable little boy. His light blue eyes had a kind of childlike calm about them too, so gentle as to be almost disconcerting. His broad clean-shaven face had none of the lines of worry and tension that Mr. Beckwith's had—no doubt, Betsy thought, because while Mr. Beckwith had to worry about him, he did not have to worry about Mr. Beckwith. It was a strong face, not weak as she had expected, and at the same time very gentle. Charles Cavanaugh's sandy-reddish hair, redder than Scott's but crisp and curly like his, was parted in the middle, which gave him a flattened open-browed appearance. He was big and broadshouldered, but very light in the way he moved, like a professional athlete who knew how to manage his bulk with ease. It was chiefly the mild ingenuousness in his face that impressed itself on Betsy. Like Scott, simple and detached and very understanding, ingenuous but not simple-minded . . . and all of it as deceptive, probably, as it was appealing, to Betsy Dayton and no doubt to all the women in creation. *It's the Irish in them,* she thought, listening to Mrs. Beckwith, but steadily aware of Uncle Charles's mild blue gaze fixed on her.

It was not too comfortable. If he had anything against her, he was being very nice about it. She might in fact have been the hibiscus, or the gardenia bush in the tub behind her. He examined both with the same placid and interested detachment.

"I'll see if your lunch is ready," Eleanor Beckwith said.

33

"My brother has a small beach house over on the Island. It's delightful, Charles—your agent did a bang-up refurbishing job for you. You must see it. Or did you go this morning?"

Charles Cavanaugh shook his head. "I sent some of my extra gear over. I hope it isn't in the way."

It seemed to Betsy that Eleanor Beckwith looked a little dubious, or even dismayed, for an instant. It passed off quickly as she said, "Scott'll be here right away, Betsy."

She was off into the house.

"There was a registered letter at Special Delivery for you, Charles," John Beckwith said. "They found it after you left the window this morning. Remarkable efficiency for them, by the way. Scott went to get it for you."

Charles Cavanaugh nodded, moving his eyes briefly from Betsy. He moved them back.

"Your father was Jerome Dayton, of Dayton Associates, wasn't he, Betsy?" he asked.

The old, familiar sensation dulling everything inside her was suddenly there once more, but heavier, because for the moment she had forgotten it. *Here it comes again,* she thought. *This is it, that's what he has against me.* She understood now, a little sick at her stomach all of a sudden. She was always trying to forget, but no one else ever did. It was all so long ago you'd think other people would forget too. But they never did. It was always the same. Always somebody looking at her and saying, "You are Jerome Dayton's daughter, are you not?" She ought to be used to it, by this time. But the sinking feeling was always there, the always being put on the defensive, all the poise and lighthearted confidence drained out of her as quickly as if someone had turned on an invisible tap. Was there something wrong with her because of what her father had done with other people's money?

I should have told Scott before I came, she thought. It had simply never entered her mind to tell him.

She raised her chin a little. "Yes, he was," she said. The necessity of keeping her voice level and matter-of-fact, so as not to sound defensive, was part of it. "Did you know him, Mr. Cavanaugh?"

"Not personally." They always said that, too. "But a friend of mine lost——"

"Betsy, Scott's here—come along, dear." Charles Cavanaugh had stopped short just as Mrs. Beckwith called from the upstairs veranda, almost as if she had been hovering there, listening, purposely breaking in. "You put the things in the carriage, Scott. I'll give Charles his letter."

Scott had come out and was up there beside her, the letter in his hand. "Hello, Uncle Charles—catch." He tossed it over the rail. It wavered in the air and glided to the flagstones, nearer to Betsy than to Charles Cavanaugh. She bent down and picked it up as he rose from his chair, her hand halting an instant as she saw the small neat colophon in the center of the gummed flat. She handed it to him.

"Thank you." He slipped it into the pocket of his slacks without so much as a glance at it.

He hopes I didn't recognize it. She had caught the flicker in his blue eyes. *And thinks I didn't.* She went past him to the stairs and stopped, smiling at him, being as casual as she could.

"I want to say one thing, Mr. Cavanaugh," she said calmly, "about what you were saying a minute ago. You know, *nobody's* friend lost anything with my father and Dayton Associates. They've all been paid back, in full. It took a long time, but it's been done."

"My dear girl," Charles Cavanaugh said quickly, "that's not——"

"If we're going to get a swim, Betsy, you'd better come," Scott called. "I'm starving."

She ran up the stairs, aware that Charles Cavanaugh's eyes were following her all the way. *He really thinks he does have something against me—or he's checking up to find out.* The heavy inlaid envelope with the neat colophon was the stationery Miles, Case and Steinberg used to answer discreet inquiries, when their regular business envelope might embarrass a client. And Charles Cavanaugh was not a client—or had not been at the close of business three days before.

But all they can tell him is what he probably knows already she told herself, puzzled. *I don't really mind at all.* But she did mind. The carefree happiness that had been in her heart was dulled and gone. The sun coming in from the street, through the hall door where Scott and his mother were stowing the lunch gear into the bottom of the carriage, with its faded pink curtains and weedy little horse, was still bright, but the ecstatic luster was gone from it, leaving it hard and brilliant and not very friendly any more. Mrs. Beckwith was laughing now, and a few minutes before had thought she was a very nice girl. What would she think when she went back and her brother held forth at lunch . . . ?

If I'd only told Scott . . . She felt suddenly very young and vulnerable . . . *It makes me look as if I were here under false pretenses.* But what could she do? She couldn't always, just because a man asked her to have a sandwich or go to a movie, say, "But you know my father was Jerome Dayton of Dayton Associates." *But I should have told him. I just never thought about it. I'll tell him now.*

That was before she saw the little man in the dirty yachting cap again.

6

Their carriage turned into Rawson Square, drowsily ringed with coconut palms, with its wooden benches across from the prim young snow-white Victoria presiding on her pedestal in front of the pillared portico of the post office and Council Chamber. The motley crew of Empire swarmed at the dock at the opposite end of the Square. Soft-voiced women with their piles of straw and shell-work sat at table stalls under umbrellas, offering their hats and baskets without insistence, in gentle contrast to the raucous naked little boys begging for coins to dive for. Porters and boatmen, their touts and hangers-on, mingled with winter residents in neat summer clothes and tourists in shorts and Hollywood shirts, under the benevolent eye of a lone native policeman in white helmet and starched white tunic.

"Uncle Charles has a boat here some place," Scott said. He helped her out of the carriage. "Ah, here's his man."

Betsy saw him then. It was the little man in the dirty yachting cap she'd seen in the carriage in Bay Street with Charles Cavanaugh earlier in the morning. He was making his way toward them, limping, his ferret-eyed hawk-nosed face pulled into a tobacco-stained, snaggle-toothed grin.

"The Boss said you and the young lydy'd be along, sir."

He touched his cap. It was clean now, Betsy saw, and his shirt was clean, and he had on clean white duck pants and new blue-and-white canvas sneakers. He was cheerful and jaunty. The shadow of death stalking him stalked invisibly, transparent in the bright salt-clean sunlight.

"This is Miss Dayton, Henry. She's not likely to want the boat alone, but if she does——"

"That's what the Boss said, sir."

Henry's cockney whine, faintly brash, sounded as foreign to the soft Bahamian-English drawl around them as the American chatter of the tourists. He darted his black eyes at Betsy and touched his cap again.

"We're just along there, sir. By the barrier."

He limped off, a boy carrying the lunch kit running on ahead.

"Henry's what you call a card," Scott remarked dryly. "But he's got a heart of gold. At least, we assume he has."

They crossed to the outer slip where the white and orange bumboats were lined up, waiting to taxi passengers over to the Island beaches or take tourists to the sea gardens outside the bay. Scott jumped aboard and held out his hand to Betsy, Henry hopping nimbly on as they pulled out of the narrow berth under the sea wall. The turquoise water was smooth and translucent as glass above the white, tide-ridged carpet of sand. Behind them the sun sparkled on the gray- and rose-colored roofs of the tiny sea-island capital secure along the sheltering slope of the low-lying hill. The houses glistened pink and white and yellow among muted reds and browns, sobered by centuries of wind and weather, in fringed palms rising above the masses of tropical green. A native sloop tacking into the wind went smoothly past them, men, women and children clustered around the smoking brazier, eating their midday meal. Sheep, chickens, piles of melons, oranges and coconuts coming into market from the Out Islands were loaded in around them until hardly an inch of freeboard was visible.

The native pilot turned. "That's why they no graveyard on Andros," he observed, and turned back to the wheel as the boat took the gentle swells feathering toward them from the sloop.

"It's so beautiful," Betsy said. "You'd think——"

Scott grinned at her. "In Nassau, you never think. You say it's picturesque and let it go at that. Otherwise you'd get sore and miss all the best of it." He was standing beside her in the stern, the chugging, evil-smelling engine sending them churning in and out among the varied craft, bumboats, yawls, yachts and ocean tankers, moving back and forth or lying at anchor in the harbor between the Islands. Then they were across the bay, slowing down, heading toward a wooden pier at the end of a narrow path, gray slate roofs shining through a jungle of tamarinds and bougainvillea and feathery wind-swept pines.

Henry reached for the wheel. "I'll tyke 'er, man. You 'op out and tyke the line. And if you'll pop out too, sir," he added to Scott. "And give Miss Dayton a 'and . . . It's a bit rough over 'ere." He brought the boat alongside and put the engine in reverse. The colored boy jumped up onto the pier. Scott stepped up after him. As he reached out to give Betsy a hand the engine speeded up, the boat lurched and backed sharply away. Betsy, caught off balance, grabbed the thwarts and hung on.

"Hey, Henry!" Scott was yelling from the pier. "Hey! What——"

"Sorry, sir—my mistyke!" Henry started back cheerfully. "Sorry, Miss . . ." The engine sputtered and went dead. He switched it on again as Betsy thought the tide would send them on the rocky shore. The boat started forward. At the same instant, she felt a sharp tug on her skirt.

"*Miss!*"

She turned quickly. The little man's ferret eyes and hawk nose were turned up toward her. The snaggle-toothed grin was gone, the urgency in his face so startling that she tightened her grip.

"Listen to me, Miss! Leave it alone . . . go back 'ome and forget it! It's not syfe!"

His voice was a hoarse whisper above the chugging engine, hoarse and desperate. "Don't s'y I told you, Miss, but get out of 'ere. You don't know 'em like I do, Miss. Don't s'y I told you, but get out quick!"

He had straightened up, looking ahead. She held on to the thwarts, still staring stupidly at him. "I . . . I don't understand——"

"Stow it, Miss." He spoke out of the corner of his mouth. "Stow it, for——sake."

He brought the boat sharply in and threw the line out, grinning up at Scott. "Don't tell the Boss, sir. 'E'd give me the sack, 'e would." He glanced around at Betsy. "Scared the young lydy. Look at 'er—pea-green, she is."

Scott Beckwith was already looking at her. "If you did that on purpose, Pop-eye, I'll beat the tar out of you," he said deliberately. "Come on now, you ape. Steady her, and quit being funny."

He reached down to Betsy and pulled her lightly up. He was still anxious and a little sore.

"I'm all right," she said calmly. "I just thought I was going to have the first swim." She smiled at him and glanced back at Henry, seeing the flicker of relief in his small bird-bright eyes.

"Sorry, Miss—my mistyke," he repeated. He hoisted the luncheon kit up onto the pier. "Do you want somebody to carry this, sir?"

"No." Scott took it. "Pick us up at five, will you, and watch yourself, you rat." He grinned down at him and took Betsy's arm. "He did scare you, didn't he, the stinker." He tightened his grip reassuringly. "But you didn't have to be scared. Henry knows his boats and engines better than he does his manners. I guess that's why Uncle Charles hangs on to him. Or I don't know any other reason."

She walked along the dry hot boards, a tight hard knot inside her. She could still hear the hoarse urgency in the little man's whisper and see the small beads of sweat on his forehead. Whatever he meant, he had meant it. It hadn't been funny. It had been frightening . . . frightening out of all proportion even to the words he'd said. If she could only know what it was even that he'd thought he'd meant . . .

"Who *is* Henry?" she asked.

"From whose point of view?" Scott asked calmly. "From Mother's, he's either the whipping boy who leads our Charles astray, or the only person who can do anything with him, except her, when he is astray. Otherwise, he's a sort of general factotum. He comes and goes. Mostly he lives in Uncle Charles's apartment in New York, takes care of him when he's there, drives his car. Ran his boat up there when he had a boat. He's been around for years. Uncle Charles keeps him on, for some reason. To do his dirty work, I guess. He's not a bad little guy, really, but he's a blasted nuisance at times."

The knot inside her had tightened again.

"What do you mean, he does your uncle's dirty work?"

Scott quickened his step. They were coming to the end of the path across to the lea side of the island. The smooth white sand gleamed ahead of them, the surf breaking in long, gentle plumes of snow. For him it was a nostalgic homecoming he never felt in Nassau itself, except for the first brief moment on the dock at Rawson Square. And coming back there with Betsy Dayton was more than just coming back.

He laughed at the earnestness in her voice. "It's just a manner of a Beckwith speaking about a Cavanaugh," he said lightly. "Uncle Charles is full of the devices and desires of his own heart. We say that, and leave it there." He looked out over the limitless turquoise of the Caribbean lying before them. "Oh, man, look at that water! We're over this way."

40

He led her along a winding path through the scrub palms and yucca to a small white pavilion.

"Ladies that side, gents this."

He stopped and lifted her chin up, smiling down into her upturned face. "Let's not worry about Henry and Uncle Charles. Let's skip 'em both. Life histories are always dull. There are other things I want to talk to you about."

He looked much more Cavanaugh than Beckwith then. She thought he was going to kiss her, and wanted him to, but he didn't, not even lightly as he had done once, and only once, before, the first night he took her home late from dinner and a movie. Perhaps that was Cavanaugh too. Give the gal plenty of rope and catch her when she falls. She moved quickly away from him into the women's dressing room across the passage. There was a staircase at the end of it leading up to the veranda and rooms overhead. At the foot of it was a wooden chest with rope handles and a faded "H. G." stenciled on the side, an expensive-looking dunnage bag initialed "C. C." propped up on top of it. The gear Charles Cavanaugh said he'd sent over, Betsy thought, Henry's as well as his own. And Mrs. Beckwith was right about the refurbishing job being delightful. The dressing room was done in pale beige bamboo with braided straw rugs and bright, chintz curtains, with mirrors and two small bars, both well stocked . . . one with a thermos jug and bottles for the inner woman, the other with oils and sunburn cream and lotions for the outer. Betsy looked at them and then into the mirror, scarcely seeing. What had Scott meant about life stories . . . and the way he'd looked at her when he said it? It was almost as if he knew she'd planned to tell him hers and didn't want to be bored listening to it. She caught herself sharply. That was more of being Jerome Dayton's daughter. Trying not to be hypersensitive, reading into simple remarks meanings that probably weren't there at all, imagining things . . .

But there was no imagining about the letter Charles Cavanaugh had slipped into his pocket, or about Henry's warning.

She closed her eyes hard shut and shook her head back and forth, trying to clear it of the bewildering maze of half-belief and half-doubt. There was something stupefying as well as frightening about all of it.

"Hey, Betsy!"

She took her beach bag off her shoulder and pulled out her bathing suit. "Coming—just one second." She undressed and

41

pulled her suit on, and then, seeing herself suddenly in half-a-dozen mirrors at once, broke into laughter. It didn't make any sense, any of it. It was all simply impossible. It was just some stupid mistake, too cockeyed even to try to understand, much less get the jitters about. She tossed her clothes onto the bamboo chair. Henry had got a touch of too much sun, or too much something else at Dirty Dick's . . . or it was two or more other people he was talking about.

7

John Beckwith looked uneasily over the steel rims of his glasses across the top of his newspaper. Always telling his wife to let her brother alone and quit worrying about him, he knew it was absurd for him to be doing it now she had gone out. Charles Cavanaugh, for one thing, was quite peacefully sunning his placid face, out at the end of the flagstone terrace. His eyes were closed and he looked as serene and sober as a baby and with every evidence of staying that way. But that was the difficult thing. You could never tell what was going on behind that amiable unlined face. He often reminded John Beckwith of Dorian Gray. Was there, somewhere, an alter-face, that recorded and revealed the ordinary human impressions of experience that the broad, ingenuously innocent, apparently real face out there seemed magically immune to? Or was it simply that Charles Cavanaugh had no conscience of any kind, so that his manifold sins and transgressions left no impression to be recorded and revealed?

Feeling the hard furrows of his own comparatively sinless physiognomy, John Beckwith smiled wryly. Then he frowned. The letter was what was worrying him. It was not like Charles to read and read again any letter, and less like him to wait till he thought he was unobserved, put his cigarette lighter to it, crumple up the charred paper and pour water on it after he had put it under the mulch in the gardenia tub. Nor was it like John Beckwith to spy on other people. But coming behind Charles to get the tobacco pouch he had left on the arm of the chair, he had been unable to avoid seeing the letterhead. He knew that first they were not Charles's attorneys and second they were Betsy Dayton's employers. It was more than odd, it was disturbing. And never what you would call voluble, Charles was still human, and his sister's comments on a girl Scott was apparently interested in, after the two of them had left for the beach, would normally have brought out some comment in return, wise or rude, depending on the girl herself or on the Cavanaugh mood. But all Charles had said was, "They're not engaged," and that was all, in spite of pressure through two courses and after-lunch coffee.

It made John Beckwith absurdly uneasy. The Cavanaughs all had a ruthless streak where women were concerned. Even Eleanor in her determined antipathy toward Andrea Huse-Lorne next door. He didn't like the idea of Scott's having it too, not where so nice a girl as Betsy Dayton was concerned . . . but if he did, his uncle would be the person to spot it much quicker than his father would. John Beckwith was not a romantic sort of person, but he knew that he had a strong feeling just then of not wanting Betsy Dayton to be hurt—not by anyone, and especially not by his son. He knew he was old-fashioned. For one thing—he understood—modern girls weren't seduced (it was even an old-fashioned word, virtually obsolete) unless they wanted it that way. His wife believed that implicitly. Charles had abundantly proved it, and perhaps Scott operated under the same rules. It was a deeper hurt than that, however, that he was thinking about. And he had the impression that she had already been badly hurt. She had the sort of sensitive, almost wistful, eagerness that he usually connected with children of divorced and unhappy parents, the fitful coming out and quickly withdrawing like the sun on an early day in spring. He glanced at his brother-in-law again. What he was thinking about was the way Betsy Dayton had instantly withdrawn when Charles had asked her if she was Jerome Dayton's daughter. He thought about the name. It was familiar, in an obscure way, but he could not place it. Her brief passage with Charles about nobody losing money with her father disturbed him too, because rude as Charles could be when he was theoretically not himself, he was never rude when he theoretically was, and naturally not to a guest in his own house.

He peered across the top of his paper again. Charles Cavanaugh was getting up. It was neither surprising nor alarming, as he could hardly be expected to lie face up in the sun all day. John Beckwith glanced around at the house. Eleanor had left him in charge, as it were . . . with instructions to keep her brother at home and straightened out, or go with him if he went anywhere. He looked back. Charles was smoothing down his hair, looping his cotton scarf around his neck and putting on the salt sack coat he had laid on the terrace wall. He was clearly going out. And there was really nothing, Mr. Beckwith reflected, that he could do about it. His sister could infringe on Charles's personal freedom if she liked, but it was hardly in John Beckwith's line.

Then he put his paper down with a suppressed groan. Charles Cavanaugh was sauntering calmly across the grass to the iron gate in the wall. John Beckwith glanced back at the house again, wishing his wife would come, and at the same time glad indeed she did not. Charles was committing the unpardonable sin, performing the final act of betrayal. The one constant and almost daily reiterated satisfaction his sister had had for five years was about to be a thing of the past. "I'm glad Charles isn't here. He'd be a perfect pushover for that woman." Mr. Beckwith grinned nervously. The cinnamon-slacked pushover was on his way. He wondered what Nell would do if he took her at her word and went along, and put the idea out of his mind at once.

"Oh no, don't disturb her." Charles Cavanaugh paused at the end of the Huse-Lornes' swimming pool, his hands resting casually in his coat pockets. His voice was raised as if Major Huse-Lorne being knock-kneed must also be deaf. "I'm sorry she's not well. I just dropped over for a moment. It's the first opportunity I've had since we've been neighbors —first time I've been in Nassau, in fact."

Ramsey Huse-Lorne untwined his long, hairy, red legs and with visible reluctance put aside the board with his half-finished game of solitaire laid out on it. He moved a black queen onto a red king before he gave up entirely.

"Do sit down," he said. "I'll get us a drink." He clapped his hands as if he were in India and there were no bells in Nassau. "What would you like?"

"Tonic water and ice," Charles Cavanaugh said. He sat down, ignoring his host's desire to be left alone to finish his game. "I also wanted to thank you and your wife——"

Huse-Lorne's jaw under the drooping points of his mustache had slackened as he took off his spectacles and put them back on with a single movement. "I say, there she is now. Better, I expect. Sun, probably. Won't carry a parasol. Frightfully energetic. American, you know."

He gave the boy in the white drill suit his order and waited for his wife, regarding his visitor with distaste. *Confident beggar. Damn well knew she'd come out. Damn well knew she couldn't resist coming now she'd brought*

45

*them to heel just to see how well they were taking it. Re-
volting business the whole thing.* And she was under the
weather, there was no pretense about that. The drawn gray-
green face glistening with beads of sweat he had seen
through the slats of her bathroom window had alarmed him,
enough for him to send her maid to see if she wanted the
doctor to come. And got no thanks for his pains.

He watched her coming down the outside staircase with
the disillusioned awareness that the presence of any male as
attractive financially and physically as Cavanaugh would
have brought her down unless she was too sick to move,
which was never the case. He looked at her anxiously, the
shock she had had not entirely worn off. She was still not
well, he could see from the hard white line around her
mouth. Her eyes that would have told him more were concealed behind a pair of those atrocious American sun glasses,
with flat, bright, green rims three-quarters of an inch wide.
They made her look like some fantastic jungle bird.

"This is Mr. Cavanaugh, Andrea."

He hung weedily in abeyance while she put out her hand,
more than delighted to meet Mr. Cavanaugh. Her scarlet lips
drawn back from her white teeth with no eyes visible to give
her smile warmth and meaning made it look almost like a
grimace, too bright and too brittle. And Cavanaugh was
quite laying it on. *Unconscionable liars, Americans. Neither
of them can be that damn-all pleased to meet each other.*

". . . very kind of you people, to take Miss Dayton in,"
Cavanaugh was saying.

"We couldn't have been happier, Mr. Cavanaugh."

Andrea Huse-Lorne crossed her elegant brown legs and
smoothed her pink linen skirt. "You have sent for a drink for
us, haven't you, Ramsay? . . . I was going to run down and
see if she was properly settled, but I had letters to write.
Ramsay's so allergic to the sun himself he thinks when I'm in
my room I must have a touch of it too. And Mrs. Beckwith
is bringing the child in this evening for a cocktail, for us to
meet." Her lips smiled. "Her name is Dayton? I don't believe
I know any Dayton, except those sweet funny things who
were here for the Miami Cup races last year. You remember
them, Ramsey?"

"Sorry," Huse-Lorne said.

"I've forgotten their names. Horribly rich, in the most
dilapidated old ketch with a coal-oil stove that blew up and
burned out the whole galley. You do remember, Ramsey."

46

"Sorry," Major Huse-Lorne repeated.

"Shipping people from Houston. Is your Miss Dayton a connection of theirs?"

"Not that I know of."

Charles Cavanaugh looked into the green-rimmed blackness that hid her eyes. Brown? Or blue?

"Her father was Jerome Dayton." He paused. "Not that you would remember."

Huse-Lorne moved uncomfortably. *No reticence, the Americans. Always explaining everybody. Walking Debretts all of them. How much money, how they made it or got it. Always parading skeletons, like dogs digging up rotten bones.* He listened to Charles Cavanaugh with one ear and with the other to the boy coming from the service quarters with the tray. At least Cavanaugh stopped talking when the servant was there. Mostly they didn't, and wondered how gossip spread.

"This is not for general consumption." Charles Cavanaugh smiled at both of them, as if to say he'd know where it came from if he heard it elsewhere. "It was a terrible thing, as a matter of fact. Her father was a chemical manufacturer. Just before our war he'd negotiated an extraordinary deal in the Argentine to build a plant and produce down there. He was flying down in a private plane, with a large sum—a very large sum—in cash, and some chemicals that commercial planes weren't allowed to carry. The cash and the chemicals were in his office at his warehouse. His secretary was there waiting for him to pick them up and take them over to the airfield. Whether she mishandled one of the cases, or the containers were defective, they never found out. The place was an inferno when the fire department got there. The watchman heard her scream, but she'd apparently locked and bolted the door and couldn't release it in time."

"Oh, I say!" Huse-Lorne exclaimed. If the beggar had deliberately set out to be offensive he couldn't have done a better job. He looked anxiously at his wife. The white hard flesh around her lips had a greenish tinge that seemed more than the reflected cast of her sun glasses. In the best of health she was psychotic on the subject of death. She refused even to allow a shilling shocker in the house. It made her simply livid for him to read one at the public library. Even Cavanaugh, the insensitive devil, ought to be able to see this was not sitting at all well.

"I do say!" he repeated.

Andrea Huse-Lorne shook her head at him impatiently. "What happened to her——"

"Her father? He came up while the fire department was there. He had a weak heart, the thing was too much for him. He keeled over dead before he got out of the taxi."

"How awful."

Mrs. Huse-Lorne put her hand out to take the glass of gin-and-tonic on the table beside her and changed her mind. She folded her hands in her lap. "How really awful!"

Charles Cavanaugh nodded. "It was, indeed. Especially as a large part of the cash that was there had been put up by friends as private investors. It had been brought from the bank that afternoon and put in the safe, and then apparently just taken out, in time to get it to the plane. It was gone, of course—the fire was uncontrollable. But Mrs. Dayton felt morally called on to pay it back. They've been badly strapped as a result. In fact, they were cleaned out."

Huse-Lorne glanced at his wife. Unlike her, he enjoyed death and disaster, vicariously, in civilized form. As she seemed interested in this case of it, there was no point in his pretending he was not.

"I say." He brightened so that not even his mustache seemed to droop so wearily. "I say, it was all explained satisfactorily, was it? I mean, no suspicion of any . . . I mean, with that much——"

"Aren't you being rather ghoulish, Ramsay?" She turned the enormous opaque blindness of her green-rimmed sun glasses on him. The hard glitter in them might have been a shaft of light on the outside of the dark glass, but it seemed to him to come through from the eyes behind. "And rather brutal too?"

"So sorry," he murmured. "I suppose I am, rather."

"As a matter of fact, it's an interesting point," Charles Cavanaugh remarked. He took the glass of tonic water beside him and swished the remaining speck of ice in it around the inside of the glass, watching it melt out of sight. "Especially as another employee of the firm disappeared at the same time and has never showed up since."

He lifted the glass and smiled at Huse-Lorne. "Well, cheers," he said pleasantly. "If it's not bad luck to say so with water, plain or tonic. I seldom touch the stuff myself."

He drank it and put the glass down. "I must get along. Nice seeing you."

As he rose, Huse-Lorne scrambled to his feet. Andrea

Huse-Lorne sat where she was, her hands folded in her lap, the smile still on her lips.

"I say, do come again, Cavanaugh." Major Huse-Lorne shook his hand cordially, as if making up for his earlier reluctance and for his wife's present failure to respond as she normally would have done. "We'll look after the young lady for you. We'll take jolly good care of her, won't we, Andrea?"

"Please do," Charles Cavanaugh said affably. "We'll be most grateful to you both." He bowed slightly, and turned back to Huse-Lorne. "I'm having a problem with the terrace wall over at my place. I wonder if I might look at yours?"

"Of course, of course."

Andrea Huse-Lorne's head turned slowly, her green-and-black owl's eyes following them down the stone steps next to the wall behind the guest cottage, her body still rigidly motionless. She waited, listening intently to the pleased babble of her husband's voice, pointing out his handiwork as rock gardener and stone mason. Her head turned back again and she reached for the bag hanging on the arm of her chair, keeping the fixed set smile on her lips until she opened it, drew out her gold compact, opened it and held the mirror up. The sun glasses had hidden the drawn tightness around her eyes, and more than that. Charles Cavanaugh had seen no knowledge in them . . . if that was why he had come. Her mouth was all she had to worry about.

She looked at it as if it were something apart from her. Then she let it relax out of the hard, fixedly-smiling lines and moistened her lips, sitting quietly there, drawn into herself, hardly moving when she breathed.

He couldn't know. There was no way of his knowing. It was all chance. There was no design or purpose in it.

Or was there? What had he meant when he said "Please do," when Ramsay said they'd take jolly good care of Elizabeth Dayton? The unctuous fool. "Please do . . ." It could have been a warning . . . a threat. Or it could have been what it sounded like—merely a polite reply to a babbling idiot. She pulled her lower lip hard between her white, even teeth and breathed deeply in and quietly out again. Cavanaugh. Charles Cavanaugh. Unconsciously she shook her head back and forth. No Cavanaugh. There was never anyone named Cavanaugh—any place, in any of it. If there had been she would have known it, no one better. She'd have remembered, when she heard his name first, when he bought

49

the house five years ago. She still remembered details then, the details she had been forcing herself to recall when she was up in her room, before she heard him asking for her, down by the pool. No, it was all in her own mind. The guilty flee when no man pursueth . . . He was simply gossiping. He believed the story the way he told it. It was the story as the newspapers had had it, and the way the family told it, no doubt. It would be the way Elizabeth Dayton would have told the Beckwiths.

Looking at herself again in the mirror, she twisted her lips into the smile she had forced and kept there. Suddenly she remembered that she must have had it there when he was telling the story . . . even when she was saying "how awful." Her throat caught and she swallowed quickly, a cold terror creeping up inside her. Could she have done that? She turned, listening intently to her husband and Charles Cavanaugh coming back up the terrace steps. Cavanaugh's voice carried across the garden, as loud as it had been when he first came and she heard him up there in her room. But it was not because he was speaking loudly. It was because sound carried up there, and because it was thrown back from the wall now. That she had to believe . . . or she was lost.

She tightened her hands on the iron arms of the chair, listening, her teeth clenched.

". . . quite a girl, actually. She has a job, with a law firm in Chicago. Miles, Case and Steinberg. Quite a good——"

Andrea Huse-Lorne's heart froze. For one long, slow instant it was dead, as still and cold as death. She rose from her chair. It was the second time that day that she had had to force herself to walk slowly, not to run, wildly, back to the awful sanctuary of her room and the hideous evidence concealed there behind the mirrored glass. It was worse this time. The mist gathered on the inside of her sun glasses blinded her, the net weaving itself invisibly around her felt so real that she stumbled, and caught herself, not daring to look around to see if they had seen her . . . no longer daring to guess what was Chance and what Design, which were the simple threads of coincidence and which the terrible strands of some inexorable fate. She had been free for so long that she had lost the technique she had perfected to gain freedom.

At the bottom of the iron stairway she turned, looking stealthily to see if the two men had been watching her. They were at the gate. Her husband's back was to her. Charles

Cavanaugh could have seen her. He was apparently interested in the wall. She breathed a little more freely as she went quickly up the stairs.

It was when she was half-way across the veranda to her room that a flash of intuitive knowledge struck her with such shocking clarity that it was physically stunning in its effect. She stood fixed to the floor, all her senses suddenly hyperacute. She saw the gooseflesh rising on her arms, noticed for the first time the paint slightly peeling on the floor, heard clearly her husband's voice and Charles Cavanaugh's, felt the renewed pulsing of her heart that seemed to have stopped as her feet had stopped. There was panic whipping it, she thought quickly . . . and there was no time for panic any more.

A trap, of course. It was all a trap. They'd set it, and she'd walked into it . . . as neatly as if she had never known there were traps.

She stood there a moment in motionless absorption, and then turned and moving quietly back to the corner of the veranda she peered down through the chink in the closed louvres through which she had watched Betsy coming into her cottage. She watched Charles Cavanaugh now without the sickening agony but with a steelier intensity, her eyes narrowed to thin slits, searching to find some line, some feature, anything, that would bring him back to her mind. He could have put on weight. His hair could have been lighter or darker. His clothes would have been different. He might have called himself by another name. Mrs. Huse-Lorne nodded slowly. There was no resemblance to anyone she knew . . . and of course—knowing what she knew now—there wouldn't be. Looking at him down there, she was seeing around and beyond him into the skilfully constructed and cunningly manipulated pitfall she had been lured and maneuvered into . . . aware at the same time that her own cunning and her own malice had been ready to their hand. If she had been watchful and alert, she would have known instantly that Mrs. Beckwith had some reason for accepting the offer of her cottage—that the fear of appearing rude would never for an instant have stopped her if she had not wanted it. She ought to have seen instantly that there was a reason for Elizabeth Dayton's being there, without having to wait until Charles Cavanaugh spoke the name of the law firm she worked for. Any fool would have known snobs like the Beckwiths would not be that pleased at their only son's

51

marrying a girl with no money and a nasty scandal in her background that not even the friendliest police were able entirely to suppress. The Beckwiths must have been used, too . . .

She looked back over the long-dead ground quietly and with a brutal and inexorable logic. There was only one answer. Jacob Steinberg must never have given up. He must have come to the inevitable conclusion that in an otherwise perfect equation, Elizabeth Dayton was the only unresolved factor . . . and using the Beckwiths, he had got her in the only position that could make her the immediate and vital menace she had become.

Andrea Huse-Lorne looked down again at Charles Cavanaugh, and brushed him coolly out of her mind. And Steinberg too. They merely complicated what was a perfectly simple matter. Without Elizabeth Dayton, they were all pawns. A sudden flash of white-hot anger shot through her as she stood there looking down at the cottage. *All right. They asked for it. Let them get it. Let them see who was the trapper and who the trapped.*

She turned with suppressed violence and stopped as she saw Charles Cavanaugh looking around toward his own side of the gate. Someone was coming from the Beckwiths'. She waited. It was only Mrs. Beckwith's maid, Rose. Mrs. Huse-Lorne watched her give the white oblong in her hand to Cavanaugh and him pass it to Ramsay Huse-Lorne, nearer the cottage. She saw her husband lean across the narrow porch and push it under the door. A letter for Elizabeth Dayton—in a legal-looking white envelope. Further instructions from Jacob Steinberg to Jerome Dayton's daughter? Mrs. Huse-Lorne smiled faintly. She glanced at her watch, wondering how long it would take her husband and Charles Cavanaugh to finish with the drainage system and move on. There wasn't too much time.

8

As Betsy Dayton started across the grass to the cottage Mrs. Beckwith stopped her. "Just a second, Betsy, there was some mail for you. Wait till I ask Rose." She turned back into the house and came out again. "She gave it to Charles. It'll be over in your room. And don't dawdle over it, darling, we're due next door in ten minutes."

As she saw the white envelope with "Miles, Case and Steinberg" on it, propped neatly in front of the mirror on the dressing table, Betsy quickened her step. Something in the office she hadn't done before she left, probably. She picked it up. It looked strange and out of place, here, with her name on it. The other letter there too was definitely strange and out of place. It was a mauve-pink square with a cluster of blue-and-yellow iris tastefully decorating the left end of it, her name and the Beckwiths' with their post office box number written in a round girlish hand in green ink across the rippling wavelets that shadowed the whole face. It was so unlike the stationery of anyone she knew well enough to get a letter from that she picked it up and turned it over. On the flap was a grinning, lop-eared face drawn in green ink, above a printed address in Oak Park, Illinois, that was as unfamiliar as the writing. She put it down, still puzzled, picked up the envelope from Miles, Case and Steinberg, tore off the end and took the letter out. Her face relaxed into a quick smile, for an instant, as she read it:

"We're counting on our girl to get her man. We miss you. It's twenty here, sleet and snow. Lucky you. Love, the Gang."

The smile faded from her face then as she looked down at it, puzzled. Was it meant to be some kind of a joke? The secretarial and clerical force at the office were anything but the Gang. They were a serious-minded lot of mostly middle-aged people who came at nine and left at five-thirty, and except for one girl, Mary Davis, who was about her own age, she knew none of them outside the office. Or inside, for that matter. And Mary Davis was the only one who knew she even knew Scott Beckwith. It must be Mary, being not funny. She smiled as she dropped it in the wastebasket and opened the second letter, expecting more of the round, girlish hand in green ink. But it was typed, three thin sheets of it, professionally typed in spite of the iris and lilies all over it. It was from Mary Davis too. The penciled initials at the bottom were familiar from the daily memos. The bewildered shadow that gathered in her eyes deepened as she read it.

"This paper my aunt gave me for Christmas is just a gag to fool anybody if anybody needs fooling. Check on the letter from the office. Look for a spot of green. I let it dry, so if it's run you'll know. This is what happened today—I guess you know what it's all about."

Betsy looked at the date and the postmark. Both were Saturday, two days after she'd left the office. It was Monday now.

"Mr. Steinberg buzzed for me as soon as his Miss E. left to go to lunch. I was just on my way out too, but he said he wanted me to take a letter. I thought it was funny but I got my book and went in. He said, 'You're a friend of Miss Dayton's, I believe.' He said, 'I clearly understood, did I not, that it was a rule of the office that no office matters be discussed outside?' Then he said, if Miss Dayton should happen to learn, without previous warning, that inquiries were being made about what she was doing in Nassau, and her reasons for being there, it might cause her undue alarm. He said he had no reason for believing she was there for anything connected with the unfortunate death of her father— sorry, honey—but that it could conceivably be dangerous for her if anyone had the impression that she was there for that reason, and he was also sure her connection with this office had not been made with the idea that it might lead her to further information about the matter."

Betsy Dayton squeezed her eyes shut and opened them, shaking her head to clear the uncomprehending fog out of them. She went on.

"He said it was regrettable she could not be apprised of the fact that inquiries were being made, and that she might possibly have given that impression, if only so she would not be placed unwittingly in danger. He said any breach of the office rules that came to his personal attention would be dealt with summarily. Then he said, any communication from the

54

office, under the firm's letterhead, to Miss Dayton should be especially guarded, so no client's affairs would be put in inadvertent jeopardy if the communication fell into other hands. Then he dictated a letter to a Mr. Charles Cavanaugh. When I brought it back he went into the same routine—it would be opposed to professional ethics for a member of the firm, and so on. Well, I'm not a member of the firm, which no doubt he knows, and he wouldn't have waited for his Miss E.—who practically thinks she is—to go out unless he had something in mind. So if you can get another address where no client's affairs will be inadvertently jeopardized, I'll send you a copy of the letter I took. I guess you know what it's all about. But it scared me, Betsy. So watch it unless you're already on your—shall we say, guard, as Mr. S. put it. So if my office letter burns you up, it's just a come-on—the way people think the office help acts. Don't think I'm trying to butt in. I'm just telling you what happened today. Good luck and love.——M. D."

Betsy held the pinkish-mauve, iris-decorated sheets in her hand for a long time, looking at them without seeing them at all. It was all so bewildering it was stupefying. She shook her head again sharply to force herself into some kind of clear reality, and picked up the tinted envelope to look at the back of it again. The grinning face was not meant to be funny. The green ink it was drawn with would have run if anyone had tried to moisten and open it, and the paper was too thin to open any other way. And the spot . . . She picked the office envelope out of the wastebasket, turned on the dressing table light, and saw it. A faint smudge of blurred green dyed the white paper at the bottom edge of the flap. She could see a crinkle where the flap had been unsealed and sealed down again, and feel it, passing her fingertips along it. It was moist, compared to the hard dry surface of the rest. Her letter from Miles, Case and Steinberg had been opened.

She held it in her hand, hearing Mrs. Beckwith's voice again. "She gave it to Charles. It'll be over in your room." Mr. Charles Cavanaugh really was making inquiries about her . . . and not only making them at the office. No stone unturned, no envelope unopened, except the obviously absurd iris-tinted job. But why . . . ? She picked up Mary Davis's letter again. . . . No reason for believing she was there for anything connected with the unfortunate death of her father —sorry, honey—but it could conceivably be dangerous for her if anyone had the impression that she was there for that reason . . . sure her connection with this office had not been made with the idea that it might lead her to further information about the matter.

What further information? What further information could she want, or hope to get, beyond the sickeningly disillusioning information she'd already got, when she stupidly decided to look up the records of her father's warehouse fire for herself, instead of going on taking her mother's story of the heart attack for granted and letting well enough alone? What other information was there? And what danger? Her body stiffened abruptly. The little man with the dirty yachting cap. "It ain't syfe, Miss . . ." She'd forgotten Henry. The sun, the sand, the cream-soft sea, Scott and the old friends of his who'd joined them on the beach, the lovely warm happiness of the afternoon, had thrust Henry and his fantastic warning completely out of her mind. She stood rubbing her hand up and down over her smooth cheek, her hand cool, her cheek hot from the sun still burning softly in it.

"I don't know what to do," she whispered soundlessly. "It's . . . it's all so . . ." She did not go on, because she didn't know what to say it all was.

She picked the letter up again. If she knew what Mr. Steinberg had written to Charles Cavanaugh, in the letter he'd slipped into his pocket, trying to keep her from seeing . . . Some other address. Her eyes brightened. She already had another address. She wasn't actually at the Beckwiths'. If she got a letter at the cottage, it could just be a mistake, by someone she'd written she was staying there who hadn't realized how close it was. That would be it. She tossed the envelope back into the wastebasket. As she did so, her eyes rested for an instant on the letter lying there, and she stopped in quick dismay. "—counting on our girl to get her man . . ." Her cheeks burned more hotly. So Uncle Charles would think she was trying to get his favorite nephew and had boasted about it in the office. She was so acutely conscious of Scott Beckwith and his casual anything-but-matrimony interest in her that any other reading of the words never entered her head; the idea of danger was too recent and still far too unreal to be half as important as the embarrassed chagrin of having Scott's uncle, and no doubt his parents, and pretty soon Scott himself, thinking she was there trying to marry him. For a moment she could have strangled Mary Davis. But it was done . . . and on second thought, not even Charles Cavanaugh was likely to broadcast information he'd got opening other people's mail.

She gave a quick tilt to her chin, picked up Mary Davis's letter, made a flat thin oblong of it and stuffed it securely under her bra. What she had to do now was send Mary a cable as soon as she could. "Having lovely time: Staying in Huse-Lornes' guest cottage." No address would be needed, in such a tiny place as Nassau.

Five minutes later she followed the senior Beckwiths, with Scott, across the garden to the Huse-Lornes' blue-tiled terrace, already dotted with cocktail-hour guests.

"I wish you knew how funny this is," Scott whispered. "Look at Ma trying to unrivet her armor plates." His voice crinkled with suppressed amusement. "If we'd known this would happen, Dad and I would have got you and Charles down here a long time ago. It's pretty childish, a couple of dames at each other's throats across a nine-foot wall. Especially when the Enemy's got a swimming pool. That's her up there in the green cheaters. Ma's sore because Uncle Charles came early to avoid the procession."

That was a relief. Betsy had come out of the cottage expecting to see him there, with the rest of them, wondering if she'd be able to watch his bland, imperturbable gaze, even considering putting on her own sun glasses. And glad now she hadn't. They had none of the brilliant glamour of the wide-rimmed, emerald-green job Mrs. Huse-Lorne had on, designed clearly to point up her watermelon-pink silk suit and balance her emerald-green platform sandals and the great cabochon emerald ring on her brown hand. Her fingers had long, watermelon-pink nails, so long they curled at the tips. The other women, including herself no doubt, looked dowdy and drab beside her, their hair dishwater dull in contrast to the sleek, shining bloom of Mrs. Huse-Lorne's.

"Such a pleasure to have you all here, Eleanor . . ."

Betsy felt Mrs. Beckwith flinch at the sound of her first name, and saw her rally Spartan-like to take a second count.

"It was so sweet of your brother to spend the afternoon with us. You know Ramsay, my dear. And is this my little guest?"

Her red lips and white teeth gleamed at Betsy, but she did not put out her hand, and Betsy's dropped back. She could not see Mrs. Huse-Lorne's eyes through the green owl's lenses, but she felt a sharp and curiously intense inventory being taken, even down, she thought suddenly, to the price tag on her nylon petticoat she had been in too much of a hurry to take off, either when she packed it or put it on. Especially at her left hand. *To see if we're engaged...* It was not only Mrs. Beckwith whose armor plate was showing, Betsy thought. Mrs. Huse-Lorne gave the impression of being brittle as vinegar taffy and as jumpy as a cat. She reminded Betsy of the two Beckwiths before Scott had explained about Uncle Charles, only not as nice and much harder. Betsy wondered about Ramsay Huse-Lorne, who was shaking her hand. Maybe he drank too, though he didn't look it. But then Uncle Charles didn't either.

"—my husband, and my son Scott," Mrs. Beckwith was saying. "I don't know if you've met before."

"Awfully nice." Mrs. Huse-Lorne was much more cordial, but of course they were men. "It's a pleasure to have Elizabeth in the cottage, Scott. I hope you'll use the pool, both of you, any time. Day or night."

Betsy heard her own first name without flinching as Eleanor Beckwith had done, but still with a little sense of surprise. No one had called her Elizabeth for years—no one ever, except her father, who had never called her anything else. Hearing it brought back the shadow. She felt the faint pressure of the folded letter against her breast.

"Will you take her around, Scott?" Mrs. Huse-Lorne was saying. "I think you know everybody. And do get a drink, won't you?"

"Right. Come on, Betsy." As Scott took her arm the shadow was gone, only to come back sharply. An elderly man, his skin so blackened with the sun that the part in his white hair made it look like a badly-made wig, came promptly up to them.

"I want to meet Miss Dayton," he said, holding out his hand to her. "—I knew your father, Betsy."

She caught her breath and kept the smile on her face, holding herself in quick tension for whatever was coming now. The man was smiling too, as Scott said a name she didn't hear.

"I want Scott to bring you over to see us," he was saying pleasantly. "My wife is sorry she couldn't come, but she wants to meet you. We think you'd like to see the house your father was going to buy for you." He smiled at Betsy's blank face. "I don't mean to be tactless, my dear," he said kindly. "But he was planning to buy our house on the Island

58

as a surprise for you and your mother. We signed the contract the morning of the day he died. He was looking forward to being here with both of you. I thought you might like to know."

"Thank you—it's sweet of you to tell me."

She could hear her voice, like Andrea Huse-Lorne's saying "Is this my little guest?" . . . with the same false syrup poured over it. He was still holding her hand in both of his, not knowing, so evidently, that her father had never intended to buy the house for her mother and her. Or maybe he had intended buying it for them, to ease his conscience and let them save face by getting out of the country when the storm broke, and he and his secretary were hiding somewhere with the money they'd stolen. She felt the flush deepen in her sunburned cheeks and tried to keep her body from quivering, because Scott still had hold lightly of her arm. Her hand in the man's warm, friendly clasp felt very dead and cold, but he still kept it.

"I want you to see the fish tanks, because they're what he was most excited about." He went on, unconscious of her flushed, unsmiling face, or too kindly misinterpreting it. "I showed him my design and my movies. I'm a fish man myself. So was he. He was as excited as a boy. You and he were going to make my collection look like a bowl of dime store goldfish. My wife couldn't interest him in the cistern under the porch, or the bathrooms or the ice box. You and himself and the fish tanks were all he'd talk about."

Her hand trembled as she took it from him. "Oh, I . . . I know he . . . he loved fish." Her voice trembled too. "We . . . we used to go to Minnesota to fish, when I was a little girl." It was the first time, for so long she could no longer remember the last, that any warm or affectionate memory of her father had come back to her, that she drew her arm from Scott's and turned her head quickly to hide the stinging moisture along her lids. She tensed abruptly then as she saw Mrs. Huse-Lorne standing only a few feet from her, staring at the three of them, the white-haired man, Scott and her. Even with the dark emerald-rimmed glasses, the odd intensity of her stare made her mouth look as if it had been set in some bitter plastic she could not make malleable enough to move if she had wanted to. Betsy Dayton caught her breath a little, flushing hotly, aware of an abrupt sheet of antagonism flaring up in front of her. Mrs. Huse-Lorne was blaming her for the silence that had fallen on the section of the cocktail party by them, as everybody seemed to have stopped talking to listen, and then had become acutely uncomfortable as they each became aware of it and started to talk at once, too brightly and too loudly. Mrs. Huse-Lorne had reason to be annoyed. But not at her—it wasn't her fault.

She turned back to the white-haired man. "Thank you so much," she said quickly. "I'd love to come. I'm sure Scott will bring me."

She slipped her arm into Scott's without realizing she'd done it, and was in effect turning to him for the confidence and support she needed, until she felt the reassuring pressure as he tightened his arm against hers. She caught herself, dismayed at her instinctive and unconscious turning to him . . . in public, and this kind of public, and tried to edge her arm away from his. He held it, talking to the man with the white hair, as detached and casual, apparently, as ever, so unobtrusively but firmly imprisoned she would have had to jerk it to get it away. She relaxed and let it stay. It was good in one way: Mrs. Huse-Lorne was much more cordial to her, all of a sudden. Or Betsy put it down to that until a few minutes later when Mrs. Huse-Lorne was showing her her deep-blue and old-gold drawing room (Major Huse-Lorne had already showed her his rock garden and drainage system).

She realized then it was no more than the old defense mechanism working again, her own false assumption that the mention of her father's name turned everyone against her. *The guilty flee when no man pursueth* . . . It flashed into her mind almost as if someone were whispering it just loud enough for her to hear. But it was Mrs. Huse-Lorne who was talking, and what she was saying was quite different.

"This Queen Anne desk is rather a dear. It was made for my husband's . . . oh, some terribly great-great-grand-mother. I never can keep up with families that go back that far." She glanced casually outside where her other guests were, and lowered her voice. "My dear, you must have thought I was being dreadfully cross, just now," she said with real contrition. "I was, but not at you—at that tactless old wretch out there. I'll never ask him to this house again. And I certainly hope you won't go over to see his house—if his ridiculous wife couldn't make a little effort to come here to meet you. I was *terribly* distressed. I didn't want you upset. You see, Mr. Cavanaugh told us about your father this afternoon . . ."

It was a stick of lightwood under the pile of brush already accumulated, flaring up in hot resentment.

"How kind of him."

It was out before Betsy realized what she was saying and how it must sound to anyone who did not realize what a meddling menace Charles Cavanaugh had become . . . or how it must sound to Andrea Huse-Lorne, until she was aware of the apparently shocked silence that lay between them. Mrs. Huse-Lorne had the advantage of the green glasses, of course, and Betsy nothing to conceal the sharp resentment blistering her own naked, brown eyes. "Oh, I'm sorry!" she said quickly. "I mean, it was kind of him."

Mrs. Huse-Lorne seemed to come to, after her shock at her guest's bad manners. She smiled, shrugging it off as one woman of the world to another. "Don't worry, darling," she said lightly. "I know precisely what you mean. But you know men. They're horrible gossips, even the best of them. Let's say he *meant* well." She laughed, making a hopeless gesture with both her hands. "Perhaps he thought it would be kind to give us some inkling, just to avoid any unhappiness for you. And of course, Betsy . . ."

She'd caught her name at once. Betsy realized her calling her Elizabeth was perfectly natural. It was curious it should have sounded so odd, as a matter of fact, or reminded her of the way her father used to say it, almost accenting the first letter instead of slurring it as most people would. Mrs. Huse-Lorne repeated it, as if she were reading her mind. "Of course, Betsy, you've got to expect a certain amount of . . . of suspicion, if not open antagonism, on Mr. Cavanaugh's part. After all, he's a wealthy man, with no wife or children. He probably feels you're trying to get his nephew, and feels he should have been consulted before . . ."

"I'm not engaged to Scott, if that's what you mean, Mrs. Huse-Lorne," Betsy said. "Or trying to get him—if that's what Mr. Cavanaugh thinks."

Not only opened my office letter and read it but broke his neck coming over to tell the Huse-Lornes what was in it. A wonderful guy but a pain in the neck to have around. How right Scott was.

Mrs. Huse-Lorne was smiling happily, her brows raised till they showed above the emerals rims of her green goggles.

"When you're as old as I am, Betsy," she said lightly, "you'll know men are much worse snobs than women ever thought of being. He's probably counted on Scott making a

61

brilliant match and holds you responsible. If men only fought out in the open . . . they pretend to, but they never do. But don't let it disturb you, my dear. You don't have to put up with him. You're in my cottage, and you stay there as long as you like. But be careful. Families have an awful way of sticking together, especially when there's money involved. And Scott . . . Here he comes—better smile, my dear."

She waved her hand lightly toward the Chinese mirrored panels on the inside wall. "And those were in my husband's family. The Chippendale frames—I had the glass put in. They were so gray and funny, when they came. You could hardly see a thing in them. It was an awful job . . . oh, Scott!" She smiled at him. "You've come to take Betsy . . . you're *not* going home! Oh, it's your parents, I know. But do come again, you and Betsy, and do use the pool. It just *sits* out there. It's been *so* nice seeing you all."

9

Mrs. Beckwith crossed the lawn ahead of them to the terrace where the maid Rose was lighting the candles on the dinner table. "Has Mr. Cavanaugh come in, Rose?"

"No, mahdam. The man say he taken the boat to the Island and not be back very soon, mahdam."

Scott Beckwith saw the instant silent fear in the subtle droop of his mother's shoulders, the line that tightened between his father's brows, and felt the familiar rise of a slow burn inside himself. It was startled out of him at once by the completely opposite effect more than obvious in Betsy. It was as if someone had cut an invisible anchor line tied to her feet, lightening her step with a sudden, eager happiness so that he had to move along to keep up with her.

He followed her, his face still soberer, wondering why the news that had so depressed the rest of them had given her such a lift. She must surely know there were people like Uncle Charles around. Go to almost any party any day, scratch a man of distinction . . . He glanced at her smiling face, mentally shaking his head. This was pretty queer. He felt a twinge of acute unhappiness. Here he'd waited to bring her down to meet his family, all because of a casual remark she'd made about a girl who was back in the office, her husband skipped off with most of her bank account. "What could she expect?" she'd asked. "She didn't know anything about him or his family. Just an attractive guy she met at the lunch counter." In a sense that was all there'd been to him—assuming he was attractive at all—he'd thought promptly, knowing then she was the girl he wanted to marry. There had never been a minute's doubt in his mind, from the day he heard her laugh as she took some letters to re-do for another girl who had a lunch date she didn't want to miss. It would be pretty funny if, after he'd hung on to himself for two long months, Uncle Charles jinxed the deal. Maybe she thought she'd inherit Charles if anything happened to the Beckwiths. Or that he, Scott Beckwith, would turn out to be a lush himself, and wanted no part of it. For the moment, seeing his mother and father valiantly pull up out of their tailspin to meet Betsy's airy level, he didn't much blame her.

But he was worried. She wasn't that strait-laced. Charles had been remarkably well-behaved all day. However, it was part of the family story that when he was on his good behavior that was just the time to hang on and watch out. He looked at Betsy again, suddenly aware this was not the first time that day—now he stopped to think about it—he'd felt vaguely that something was wrong. He'd brushed it off before, knowing she really was delighted with the place. He couldn't have brought anybody there more excited or entranced or amused by the whole thing—the color, the people, the native shops in the market, the kids diving for pennies, the straw market. She'd loved it. And then, all of a sudden . . . He fished around in the pool of the half-forgotten day. The first time he'd noticed it was when Betsy came up to get in the carriage to go to the Island. The second was after Henry had done his curious trick with the boat, when they were crossing to the pavilion. He frowned a little. It seemed to make Charles the only common denominator in one form or another, as she'd bucked up, all of a sudden, after the cocktail party, when he wasn't present. But she was calling him to dinner, now, so entirely herself that he decided maybe he was imagining things, hypersensitive because he wanted so much for her to be happy there, and in a frame of mind where she'd listen to all the things he wanted to say to her.

He let it go out of his mind only to have it come back, gnawing at him again, after dinner when the two of them set out to go down to the cable office. Memories of himself as a kid, sending his parents a wire to make up any excuse to spring him from places where he was an unhappy guest, flashed irresistibly into his mind as he stood outside the Telecommunications Office, lighted up like a penny arcade in the dark narrow street. He wanted to tell her that, but something in her lilting step as she came out of the bare white building made him change his mind. It looked too painfully near the truth for him to take the chance, and she was too happy again for him to risk spoiling the warm responsiveness of her hand in his as they crossed the street to the Carlton House patio.

A blind man with a guitar was singing.

"Dance, gal, dance,
Sponga money easy come,
Sponga money never done . . ."

"That's the saddest song in the Islands," he remarked as they went inside. "Sponges were the natives' big cash crop—all died out with a fungus . . ."

As he turned to her he saw she was not listening to him or to the melancholy, plaintive music. She was standing there stock-still, looking through the window into the Bar, the light gone out of her face, her lips parted. He looked past her and saw Charles Cavanaugh. He was sitting at a table against the wall, leaning forward in deep and earnest conversation with Henry. The little man was hunched forward, his cap pushed back on his head, his eyes fixed on the diagram Charles Cavanaugh was drawing with his wet forefinger on the table. They were both sober, the ale in their glasses as dead as ditchwater.

She turned quickly. "Let's not stay here. We can hear him sing some other time. Let's go somewhere else. Or let's go home—I'm dead. I need some sleep."

She moved back, her smile too bright, evidently not knowing he had seen them. He followed her in a half-dazed process of waking up to something with no idea of what it was. Except that she was violently opposed for some reason to Charles Cavanaugh. She was almost running. As they came to the corner he saw her face more clearly, and caught her arm.

"Betsy! What's the matter?"

"Nothing. I'm just tired. I didn't know how tired I was. I'd just like to go back and go to bed, that's all."

He could see now she was frightened, and he should have seen it before. She looked the way she'd looked on the boat with Henry. "Pea-green, she is, sir." He tightened his grip on her arm.

"Betsy . . . has my uncle . . ."

She looked up at him with blank wide eyes. "Oh, don't be silly," she said quickly. "I did see him in there, but that isn't why I didn't want to go in. I really am a wreck, Scott. Just think how many thousand miles we've been the last twenty-four hours."

What she had seen through the window was blazing in her

mind. The diagram Charles Cavanaugh was drawing, the wet lines shining on the table top. A diagram of the Huse-Lorne cottage, and the grounds. The tiny building, the wall, the gate in the wall, the steps leading up behind it from Huse-Lorne's rock garden, the cistern built there to catch the water for his flowers . . . Huse-Lorne had showed her at the party. He had showed it to Charles Cavanaugh earlier, he'd said. "Mr. Cavanaugh is really interested in my system . . ." With Charles Cavanaugh's moist forefinger tapping on the square spot in the diagram that was the cottage, while Henry slowly nodded his head, it all added up to something that for an unreasoning instant made her sick with sudden icy terror.

She hurried breathlessly along now, forgetting Scott was there beside her. How many times, by how many people, did you have to be told it wasn't safe? The little man's hoarse whisper. Mary Davis. Mr. Steinberg. "It's not syfe, Miss." It scared her. She might be unwittingly in danger. All because somebody thought she knew something, or was trying to find something out, about her father's death that she didn't know at all and wasn't trying to find out . . . but was beginning slowly to wonder about.

"I'm terribly sorry—but you don't mind, do you?" she said. "I really have to go and get some sleep."

"Of course not, Betsy." She was lying, he knew helplessly. He had no idea of what to do. "It's just Nassau," he said, as lightly as he could. "The salt air, sudden change of tempo. Lets you down fast the first day. You'll feel swell tomorrow."

He waited at the cottage door until she had opened it and turned on the light. "Good night, Betsy."

"Good night."

He waited again as she closed the door, and listened to the soft click of the key turned in the lock, swallowing the unhappy taste in his mouth as he turned back to the iron gate. She had never left him so quickly before. The warm lingering that was about the only tangible thing he had to show he was gaining any ground at all was acutely absent, and his resentment lengthened his stride across the lawn and through the quiet house out into the street. Down the hill and along Shirley Street was the shortest way back to the Carlton Bar.

Ramsay Huse-Lorne let his hairy sun-reddened hands

droop flaccidly over the arms of his old wicker study chair. He was in his own room among his own worn possessions— the last stand against the crass newness his wife and the decorators had managed to invest everything else with that had belonged to him. New glass for old in the Chippendale mirrors, new gilt and new varnish on the portraits, new polish on the Queen Anne desk. He sat there under his green shaded gooseneck reading lamp, gazing with fixed concentration on the game of solitaire he had started when Cavanaugh interrupted him and was going to finish before he went to bed. The black eight of spades clearly did not belong where he had put it, on the red ten of hearts. He realized it, and realized at the same time that he had had rather more to drink, beginning with Cavanaugh's visit, through the cocktail party, and afterwards, than was reasonable. He would have been all right if he hadn't given in to the violent desire to get out of the house and out of sight of Andrea, purring like a jungle cat with her triumph over her neighbors and their friends. And all right then, if he hadn't run into Cavanaugh in Bay Street and gone to the Carlton Bar with him. Damn the fellow. But it was himself he was thinking about. He had made a hysterical ass of himself, suddenly cracking up and pouring his heart out, as if Cavanaugh were the confessional or his oldest friend. He'd like to think it was Cavanaugh pumping him, about his wife and all the rest of it, but he knew that if that had been the case he would never have opened his mouth. It was far-fetched, even in his present less muddled state, to believe Charles Cavanaugh was remotely interested in where and how Ramsay Huse-Lorne had met and become engaged to his wife. Or the sort of person she appeared to be then—in appalling contrast to the one she turned into when a new governor's wife took her up, largely to spite the older more staid residents who didn't flock about as quickly as they might. Or that Cavanaugh could be interested in the Huse-Lorne financial problems.

Major Huse-Lorne suppressed a miserable groan. He couldn't understand what had got into him, bleating like a wretched fool, started off after Cavanaugh had bought him several drinks and he offered to buy the next one before he remembered he had no money and didn't dare risk asking to sign another chit. Money, money . . . that was what had set him off on Andrea, the frail, helpless little widow who needed a strong honest man to take care of the little her late husband had left her, and had turned into the Andrea who had all the strong, honest and not-so-honest men backed clean off the board when it came to buying and selling and multiplying what she had several times over, sitting tight when British flight capital started in after the war and then managing to clean up a good bit of it too. And raised such living hell whenever he got so fed up he tried to get a job of work to do, that it was easier to stay on short rations than have her make a laughing-stock of him everywhere they went.

He cringed, realizing he had made one of himself to Charles Cavanaugh, who'd been damned decent to listen to him and not chuck him out into the road on his backside as he ought to have done. And if the little Cockney boatman hadn't come along, he'd probably still have been there, bleating like a pauperized victim of the Socialist Government, the way so many of his self-exiled countrymen did. They at least had the grace to bleat about the Government, not about their wives. Huse-Lorne's chin sank lower into his clavicles. He blinked myopically at the card he still held in his hand. The eight of spades. The death card . . . The lady fortune-teller at the Red Cross Bazaar at Government House last week—the horse-faced woman with the mole under her chin—had called it the death card. Waved it under his nose. "You'll hear of a death shortly, Major. Not your own— you're way over here out of reach." He turned the card face over on the board and blinked again. Then he picked it up and looked at it. Nonsense, of course, but rather horrible nonsense. His eyes moved across the room to the writing table against the wall. The letter he'd left for his wife to read before he went to the bathing pool was there, where he'd put it, after finding it where he'd left it in the drawing room. She hadn't even bothered to read it. Somehow he was very glad she hadn't. The fact that a frail old man was dying wouldn't interest her, except as it moved him to where Mrs. Huse-Lorne became Lady Huse-Lorne. But the plea for £50 to keep the old Tory from having to accept State Medical care would have seemed excruciatingly funny to her. That, it would be hard for him to hear, hearing her already in his mind. "The Marshall Plan pays for it, doesn't it? Why does he beg from me? Let his Government beg for him." If she said it once again, Ramsay Huse-Lorne knew he would kill her.

He let go the eight of spades as if the temptation was already burning his hand. It dropped on the floor as he got up, went over to the bureau and opened the bottom drawer. There was a battered, japanned strong box in it. He took it out, got the key from his stud box, opened it, took out the small packet of notes under the papers on top and counted them. There was still only forty-two pounds. If Andrea had left it there, it would have been eighty-four by this time, he thought with a twitch of one eyelid. He put it in his pocket. It wasn't fifty, but it would have to do. He'd won it at roulette at the Bahamian Club, the only luck he'd ever had, when Andrea was visiting on Eleuthera.

He closed the box and slipped it hastily back into the drawer, listening toward the balcony. He thought he heard her coming. She was in her room—he'd seen her light when he came in. He went quietly across the room and switched out his own light. The green cast onto the balcony disturbed her, she said, in her repeated attempts to make him discard the beaten-about, old gooseneck reading lamp he had had as long as he could recollect. He waited in the dark, for the luminous starlit curtain the night would raise along the open balcony when his eyes became adjusted enough to see it. He reached down, took off his shoes and crept over to the screened French windows. Andrea must have gone to sleep. There was no light from her door. He listened again, then went quietly out onto the veranda and stood looking down into the garden.

The pool shimmered softly through the long, feathering palm leaves. Somewhere to the right, a blopping thud startled him until he realized it was only a coconut falling to the dry ground. He glanced down at the cottage, wondering whether Miss Betsy had been startled by it, if she was awake, or if she was in yet. An attractive girl. He looked back at the pool, and cautiously around at his wife's dark windows. A cool bathe would soothe his rather swinish head, he thought. If Andrea heard him, she'd think it was young Beckwith and the girl she'd so cordially invited to use it any time, day or night. His using it at night she seemed to consider a personal offense, sure to give them both malaria. He realized he must still be slightly squiffish even to think of disobeying her edict. Nevertheless he felt his way back into his room, turned his light on again, went into the bathroom, put on his black bathing drawers and got himself a dark green towel off the rod. If he slipped down the service stairs, she would not awaken at his shadow passing her windows.

He came back across the heavy grass rug, stepped on

something cool and smooth and realized as he reached the door that it was sticking to his bare moist foot. He raised his foot and peeled it off. It must be the card he had thrown down, the eight of spades. Death sticking to him like a brother. He tossed it away and went on down the servants' stairs.

10

Betsy woke out of a hag-ridden slumber and looked again at the traveling clock on the table by her bed, watching it heavy-eyed to see if the hands were still moving in response to the muted tick-tick she could hear in the blank dead silence of the room. The bright pointer stepping from thirteen through fourteen to the quarter mark past one o'clock convinced her that it was, and she turned her head back and closed her eyes again. It was the longest night she had ever spent—and more than one-half of it was yet to come. From a quarter past ten she seemed to have lived a hundred leaden-weighted hours, interspersed with sleep that was worse than waking. It was sleep filled with formless terrors that vanished just as she seemed about to identify and give a name to them, and she found herself awake, cold sweat drenching the sheet that covered her.

And awake, she was back face to face with the sickening mess she had made of everything. She had been a fool from the very beginning of it, a fool to come, a fool ever to let herself fall in love, a worse fool to let Scott see how she felt about his uncle. The way she had left him on the porch, and the way he had left her . . . "You don't mind, do you?" "Of course not, Betsy." Why should he mind? You bring a girl to Nassau to have some fun and she turns out to be a cold, wet fish for no reason whatsoever. She's tired. She wants to go to bed. Okay. No wonder he was glad to let her go, so he could find somebody who wasn't tired, who did want to stop and listen to the man sing, who'd be delighted to go into the bar where his Uncle Charles was.

The sickening wretchedness in her heart, from the moment she'd closed the door and heard him stride vigorously off and she was alone in the silent room, drowned out all the rest of the incredible unreality of the day, thrusting it aside to emerge only when she dropped off into a moment of disturbed and restless sleep. She squeezed her eyes shut, wishing the tears would come normally and let her rest, instead of her mouth being flooded with a salty, unshed taste that kept her swallowing in a misery of unrelief. She moved her head back and forth on the pillow. She had been such a fool—she'd better go home the way they must want her to go home, and forget all about it, about Scott and about everything that had suddenly lifted her up and made her life a glowing, dancing dream. "It's Nassau . . . you'll feel swell tomorrow." If she could only skip tomorrow, skip it and get out before she had to face any more of Scott's off-hand disillusionment . . . and have to face his Uncle Charles, with his bland quiet gaze.

The clock had hardly moved, when she stared miserably at it again, and she sat up abruptly. She'd been a fool, but she was being a bigger one now. It was because she was tired and pulled to pieces that it all looked much worse than it really was. If she could only get some sleep and wake up without looking like a lost owl with deep circles under her eyes. She reached her feet into her slippers on the floor beside the bed. The ache in her heart had translated itself into a dull, throbbing pain in her temples and the muscles of her eyes. Too much sun, probably, after the troglodyte existence she'd been living at home. If she took an aspirin . . .

She reached over to turn on the light, and decided against it. It must have been turned on and off a dozen times already, in the last three hours, and she remembered now that the two houses, the Beckwiths' and the Huse-Lornes', with their screened bedrooms on the open verandas, looked directly down on her. They'd think she never settled down, if her light kept going on and off, waking them every five minutes. And the filmy glow of the starlit night sifting in through the tilted slats of the venetian blinds made it light enough to see anyway. The aspirin were in her dressing case on the stand in the bathroom. She felt her way across the tiled floor and went inside. It seemed darker there, with the vines shading the window, but she knew where the bottle was in the dressing case tray. She felt about there until she came to it.

"You should never take anything without looking first to be sure it's what you think it is." As the words flashed into her mind she smiled in spite of her aching head. How many times had her mother's sleepy voice told her that, when she tried to get in and out of their small bathroom at night without waking her? She unscrewed the bottle cap, reached to the washbowl to turn on the water and remembered that both Scott and his mother had told her not to drink the tap water in Nassau. There was bottled water in the thermos by her bed. She started back to her room and stopped, her head turned to the open window, listening.

There had been so many unfamiliar noises against the deepening silence of the last couple of hours, after the sound of native voices singing lusty hymns somewhere to a hot wheezing organ had broken off—leaving a void as sharp as if someone had turned off a blaring radio on a country lane— that she had found herself constantly startled. But this was different. Not the rustle of the palm leaves, or the dull thud of coconuts dropping that Major Huse-Lorne had told her not to be alarmed about. Nor a vine whispering as it scraped the bright rough stucco on the outside wall. It was something else. She shut her eyes and listened intently. A low snarling whine, like that of an animal, came to her ears. It turned abruptly from a snarl into a savage half-whisper. It was not an animal. It sounded like two people quarreling there.

She opened her eyes, drew back toward the door and stood there, her hand on the light switch, hesitating. If she turned it on . . . It was quieter then. They were going away. She could hear soft footsteps, going down the steps cut into the rock of the grade, along the side of the cottage, silently, rubber or rope-soled feet. She listened. The maid, perhaps, slipping in late to her room below, though she did not hear a door open or close. It didn't really matter. If it was anyone it shouldn't be, it was the Huse-Lornes' problem, not hers. She put the aspirin bottle on the table, started to pour a glass of water out of the thermos, and realized suddenly that her head had stopped aching. She managed a smile. Just thinking about something not herself for a moment had been all the analgesic she needed. She sat down on the side of the bed, pulled her feet out of her slippers, reached to get the sheet to smooth out its disordered knots, and stopped again, sharply startled at a new sound coming through from out of doors. She went quickly over to the window, her heart a lump lodged at the bottom of her throat, the panic and the alarm all there again, and reached for the cord of the venetian blinds. The thudding noise, out of the silence out there, and the splash . . .

Then she dropped her hand and breathed deeply, relieved and a little ashamed of herself. The place was silent as the tomb again, nobody else even awakened by the thudding sound and the splash. She could see the lines of shining, rippling water of the swimming pool glittering like a ladder through the slats of the blind, the slanting shadows of the palm tree splintering the even strips into broken moving steps. Major Huse-Lorne had warned her not to be alarmed. "Makes a frightful din till you get used to it, Miss Betsy. Thub, splash. It's a double hazard, really." He was pointing to the coconut palm leaning gracefully over the corner of the pool, the fruit in a heavy, dark cluster under the pale, lovely frond and bract of the new blossoms above it. "If you don't drown normally, a coconut bounces on your noggin and knocks you up so you drown anyway. I keep telling Andrea we ought to cut the wretched thing down, it fouls the pool most frightfully. But don't be alarmed if you hear 'em bopping and splashing about in the middle of the night, will you." She smiled, remembering him. He sort of bounced up and down when he talked, as if his knees were made of rubber or had oiled springs in them.

She went back to her bed and pulled her feet in under the sheet. It was then she saw the faintly gray-white object on the dark tile just in front of her door. She stared down at it, straining her eyes. It looked like a note stuck through under the door. She straightened up, her mouth suddenly very dry, sat looking at it for an instant, then brushed the sheet aside, ran across the room and picked it up.

Major Huse-Lorne's black bathing drawers were still dry, the dark towel around his bony torso helping them in giving his red-white skin the camouflaged effect of light and dark that concealed him against the mottled shadows of the sago palm between the service quarters and the pool. It was as far as he had got before he realized he was not alone in the garden. There was someone on the other side, near the cottage. His first impulse was to call out. He stifled it at once, not wishing to alarm either his wife or Betsy Dayton. Also, without his distance spectacles he was not able to see clearly, and it might be Miss Dayton herself, with young Beckwith, just getting in. He peered through the shadowy thickets of the shrubs and vines growing against the wall and over it. It was rather curious. He felt he could sense, even if he could not see, that it was not a trespasser or simple intruder. One of the Beckwiths coming for a bathe, no doubt. In the still foggy state of his mind it did not seem too extraordinary. In fact it seemed eminently reasonable, as he was out there himself for the same purpose. What did seem peculiar was

74

the silence over there. It occurred to him again that he should sing out. He dismissed the idea abruptly when he saw the second figure. It was a woman. She seemed to appear from nowhere, almost as if she had materialized out of the shadows, having been until then a living part of them.

Major Huse-Lorne shifted his weight uncomfortably and eased himself deeper into the shadow of the palm. It was extremely awkward. He didn't wish to spy on their guest. On the other hand, it was definitely not in keeping with his whole sense of order and decorum. It was more than that. In a kind of muzzy and unreal fashion, he was aware that this was not a lovers' meeting . . . and the girl, or woman, had not come out of the cottage at all, or even appeared from the direction of the cottage. It was disturbing. It was also extremely bewildering. The only other woman there was his wife, and the idea of Andrea coming down to meet anyone in the garden at this time of night was too palpably absurd to consider. Andrea did not like the dark. It made her uncomfortable, even when she was with other people. And if it was not Andrea, then it must be the Dayton girl. But the man was not Scott Beckwith. Beckwith was tall and well set up and Major Huse-Lorne's impression now was that the woman was the taller of the two people he had indistinctly seen.

He glanced uncomfortably back the way he'd come. It was deuced awkward, all round. If he had returned at once it would have been all right, but it was impossible now, without a serious risk of being seen or heard. In any case, since he was unable to hear what the two of them were saying, or see clearly enough to identify them, he was not actually eavesdropping. He considered that carefully, with no thought that he was being absurd, or other than a man with certain standards living up to them as well as possible under the embarrassing circumstances in which he found himself. He was relieved, at last, when he saw the two of them were moving off from where they had stood. The girl would go back to the cottage, the man . . . But he was wrong. They both went on, the woman leading the way. He could see the indistinct silhouette of her dark cloak against the pale stucco of the cottage as she went silently past it, down the rock-ledged steps. And the man . . . Huse-Lorne frowned. Some yachtsman, it was. Or a boatman. He caught the faint gleam of a white-topped cap. He remembered suddenly that the maid was sleeping down in the lower level of the cottage, and had a moment's sharp relief until he saw or heard nothing to indicate the girl had gone back inside, and remembered then that Andrea had let her go to see her children who lived with her mother on Andros.

He had turned to go back to the house when he remembered that. He stopped, more puzzled and disturbed than before, torn between reluctance to seem to pry and a feeling that it was his duty to investigate. He decided to let well enough alone and go back to the house, and he was halfway up the service stairs when he heard the hollow splash across the garden.

He continued on for a step, and then, as the sound of it focused more sharply in his mind, he stopped and stood where he was, half expecting to hear a shout and ready to dash back down the stairs when he should hear it. Not hearing a shout or call, he went down the stairs anyway, stepped out onto the narrow service porch and stood there peering out, his jaw drooping vacantly. Damned curious, Major Huse-Lorne thought. He waited. There was no sound. He stood there for a moment, undecided. He'd look an awful ass if he went out there now, he thought, glancing down at his costume and a little startled by it, now that he was quite sober and in his right mind. He hastened back up the stairs, suddenly embarrassed at what he might have looked like, running berserk through the grounds, his disordered fancy always jumping to bizarre and ridiculous conclusions. If Miss Dayton wanted help, she had three stout fellows to supply it, the two Beckwiths and Cavanaugh. He flushed furiously, remembering Charles Cavanaugh and only dimly remembering now the long tale he'd been telling him at the Carlton Bar.

He had got to the top of the stairs and started to go along to his room when he turned and looked down into the garden. He took a breath of deep relief that he hadn't gone barging out there. Miss Dayton was back in the cottage. He saw the light go up in the bathroom window. He started to move around the mat screen to go to his room when he stopped short, completely dumfounded. The light was on in Miss Dayton's room, but the woman he had seen was still out in the garden. She was directly below him, alone, coming toward the house, coming swiftly and silently.

Ramsay Huse-Lorne's jaw dropped sharply and his weak eyes bulged as he saw her come quickly around and slip into the stairway at the other end of the veranda. It was Andrea.

He could hear her soft rapid tread on the stairs and the faint metallic clink of the iron as it vibrated with the weight and speed of her body in flight upward. She was at the top. He could hear the difference in the sound of her feet as she reached the porch and came across the tiles, and again the difference as she got to the grass rug. For one instant, something very odd happened to Ramsay Huse-Lorne. He thought she was coming to his door. Coming to him for help. A sudden extraordinary and overwhelming incandescence shot up inside him. He would help her. Whatever she'd done, he would help her—more than gladly. The flame had shot up, it burned down and died out as instantly. She was not coming to him for help, or at all. She had stopped at her own door and slipped inside as swiftly and stealthily as a cat.

Major Huse-Lorne stared blindly into the mat screen concealing him. He turned, suddenly sick with horror, and went silently back down the stairs.

Betsy Dayton picked up the folded white paper barely visible at the bottom of the door. She held it for an instant, a sudden eager hope lighting inside her. Perhaps Scott . . . She went breathlessly into the bathroom and switched on the light, closing her eyes for a moment against the intense brilliance that hit her almost like a blow after the interminable darkness . . . He must have felt something, if she had felt so much . . . She blinked her eyes, adjusting them to the light as her hands opened the folded paper. She looked down at it, and saw what it said, not word by word but all of it at the same time, all in one incredibly stunned and terrified glance.

"Warning," it said. "Dont take no pills. That's how they killed your father."

11

How long Betsy Dayton stood there staring down at the sheet of letter paper in her hand, how many times she read the message written on it, she could not have told. Time seemed to have dissolved into nothingness, leaving her suspended, motionless, in a spacial unreality that was like a trance state, devoid of all sensation and all emotion. A sound from somewhere far off outside the room brought her gradually back. The pink, tiled walls of the bathroom slowly closed in to their places, and she became aware of them, as if they had also dissolved into nothing and emerged into reconstructed being again. She saw the paper in her hand as something physically real, saw the ragged edge at the top where the letterpress had been clumsily torn off and saw the words, themselves as apart from their meaning. They had been scrawled across the soiled paper with a scratching, spluttering pen, their shadowy inverted forms making a gaunt skeleton under the crease, where the paper had been folded while the ink was still wet and the words imprinted a second time.

Her hand reached slowly out and switched off the light. She moved back into her room to the side of the bed and sat down.

"Warning. Dont take no pills. That's how they killed your father."

The paper, the words, the blurred stipple around the words where the pen had scratched and spluttered, were a vivid after-image still indelibly printed on her retina, the whole note a symbol she no longer needed to see now to be able to read. She sat there intensely quiet, her mind reaching in and out, alert but strangely composed and quiet too. The aspirin tablets were on the table less than two feet from her. She could turn on the lights, take the bottle, dump the tablets out and read the tiny label on each one, if she chose. But they were not important. They could wait till tomorrow. The rest of it was the important part.

Her father had not killed himself. He had not deliberately taken the cyanide tablet that killed him. Someone—*they*—had put it where he would take it . . . as they might have put it in her aspirin bottle and she might have taken it a little while ago, and been written off a suicide herself—like father, like daughter. It seemed strange to her, sitting there in the luminous half-dark, that she could look at all of it as calmly and without emotion as she was doing. It could be because she was so shallow she had no more emotion left, after the last few hours. But she knew that was not so. It wasn't that. It was something very different, that she recognized because, in small ways, she had been through it before. The knowledge of reality was far easier to bear up under than the blind ignorance of doubt and apprehension. Present fears are less than horrible imaginings . . . And in a larger sense she knew this was a confirmation of something she had in some profound way known, but had been stunned into loudly denying when the apparent truth had shocked her so bitterly, as she read the files that closed the police inquiry into her father's death. All that day she had kept her mind shuttered, with an adamantine blindness, refusing to see what was so clearly obvious, that her having done that was more shocking to her now than the truth confirmed. The Why of it, why she had wandered, why she had now been led into the pathway of understanding, was still outside the limits her mind was reaching for. But the practical, immediate things were very clear.

It was Henry, of course, the limping little Cockney boatman, Charles Cavanaugh's man, who had written the note and put it there. He'd warned her in the boat, he was warning her here again. It would have been him she'd heard outside, the snarling whine that had made her think at first of some animal. But there'd been two of them. He'd been quarreling with some one . . . Her mind moved around Charles Cavanaugh, avoiding the final step that must bring her to him. She turned her eyes to where the dressing table was, across the room. Mary Davis's typed letter on the iris-covered mauve paper was in the drawer where she'd put it, between her handkerchiefs in the blue-satin lingerie case. The salty taste flooded her mouth again and she swallowed and looked away. What did it mean? Why did Charles Cavanaugh inquire of her employers why she was coming down there? How did he even know who she was? What knowledge could he have, unless he had more knowledge than he should have had? But then why should Henry, Charles Cavanaugh's man, have warned her, in the afternoon and again here?

A sudden, painful twist inside her made her get up and move abruptly to try to dislodge it. All the years, her mother, and all the rest of them who had known, had believed as she had been doing, that her father was a thief, a treacherous scoundrel . . . and finally a coward. No one remembering anything decent about him, burying his memory in silence and oblivion, writhing with shame whenever his name was mentioned. It was hideous. The elderly white-haired man, the man that afternoon, with his skin so sun-blackened his hair looked like a wig, was the only person she had ever heard say anything kind about him—except her mother, trying with a forlorn desperation to keep the truth from her, until she went out and found it for herself. And it had not been the truth at all. The pain writhed inside her. The truth was murder . . . still hideous and awful, but better than the other.

She started to go over to the window and stopped abruptly, stumbling against the chair in front of it and straightening up, staring blankly ahead of her. She was going at the whole thing backwards . . . it was herself and her mother she was thinking about, not her father. But . . . if he had not taken his own life, as the police reports said . . . If he had been murdered, it was by someone, for some reason. The reason would have been the money, that was burned in the fire . . . For an extraordinary moment she stood there, stunned by the clarity of the new picture before her. The fire . . . Miss Gurney . . . Her lips moved, pronouncing the name. Her hands had gone cold and her lips dry. *Then Miss Gurney must have been murdered too.* The shocked, living horror that she had not felt when she read the message surged over her. Miss Gurney was murdered too.

She sat down in the chair by the window and put her hand up to her mouth, covering it almost as if she were stifling a shocked cry. Miss Gurney and her father . . . *They had not been going away together.* Of course they had not. That had been the most unbearable part of it, for her mother, and the hardest and most unbelievable part of it for her, when she had finally learned. Miss Gurney had been so old, and so unattractive, her father always so irritated at the sloppy clothes she wore. Shadowy, long-forgotten pictures came drifting back into Betsy's mind, of her father's office in the warehouse, where he used to take her and let her do her arithmetic on the machines in the bookkeeper's small office next to the fireproof steel door into the laboratory where all the smells were. She pressed her fingers hard against her temples, trying to remember, and released them suddenly, turning her head to the window.

Someone was out there again. She rose quickly and looked out between the slats of the venetian blinds. It was Major Huse-Lorne. He was in his dressing gown and pajamas.

She pushed her hair back from her forehead, bewildered, and watched. He was coming up from the lower terrace, cutting across the garden toward the house. She followed his lank figure across the terrace. The lights went on in the drawing room. She saw him cross the room as if it were a lighted stage, and disappear from sight. Her heart beat quickened with an apprehension she did not understand. Then she saw him again. He came rapidly out of the lighted room and turned up the stairs, leaving the lights on. A second later she saw another light. It was on the veranda, in the room where she had seen the maid stop with the tray that afternoon, stop and go away again. Jezebel's room, she had decided it was, using the Beckwiths' term for Andrea Huse-Lorne. It showed you ought to know people before you took other people's estimate of them, she thought, forgetting her own first estimate of Mrs. Huse-Lorne. She couldn't have been kinder or more understanding, actually. It brought her back to Charles Cavanaugh, and she looked down at the note that had fallen from her hand when she stumbled against the chair. She picked it up quickly and folded it into a small square. The problem was getting to be where to keep things where Charles Cavanaugh couldn't find and read them. Before she slipped it into the pocket of her pajama top and moved back to the bed she looked out of the window again. There were more lights at the Huse-Lornes'.

The puzzled lines deepened between her brows and she felt the nameless apprehension again. She shook her head slowly in the dark room. It must have been a coconut falling into the swimming pool. The only other place where there was water was the cistern down on the lower terrace where Major Huse-Lorne collected rainwater for his garden. It had been covered with a wooden top, when he showed it to her,

81

lifting it for her to look down into the dark, glistening chamber under the flagstones.

Ramsay Huse-Lorne paused only a brief instant outside his wife's bedroom door on the veranda, brief in time but immeasurable in terms of the staggering, emotional shock he was undergoing. There was *some* explanation. There had got to be. It must have been his own horrible imagination, acutely disordered, some way, by the fantastic euphoria of intoxication. He must have been far more in liquor than he had thought. But there was no time to think now, and he paused not to try to think but to give himself a final jerk together so as not to let Andrea see the hideous conflict that was shaking him. The swan's neck handle of her door felt cold and clammy in his hand as he took hold of it.

"Andrea!" he whispered sharply. Why did he whisper? It sounded hoarse and alarming even in his own ears. He rattled the screen, latched securely from the inside. "Andrea!" he said. The sickening dread curdled inside him. She couldn't be that soundly asleep so quickly. He thrust the thought from his mind. It was contemptible of him to think in such terms.

"Andrea!" he repeated. He knocked firmly on the door, and heard her turn over in bed.

"Yes?" Her voice was heavy with sleep. "Ramsay?"

He heard her fumbling for the light on the table by her bed, and saw her, blinking and twisting her head against the double impact of waking and the light. She straightened herself against the satin quilted headboard and looked around at the door into the hall, then peered forward, blinking out toward him.

"*Ramsay?* What on earth are you doing out there? If you want to come in, can't you come in properly? What is the . . ."

"Open the door, Andrea," Huse-Lorne said quietly. "I've called the police. They'll be . . ."

"You've called *what?*"

She was out of bed and across the room, unlatched the screen and pushed it open. Her body stiffened as she drew aside for him to come in. Her eyes contracted, as sharp as her voice. "Have you been drinking?"

"Yes. That's not the point."

He didn't look at her. He went over to the chaise longue and picked up her tailored, blue-crêpe dressing gown. "Put this on. The police will be here in just a moment." He handed it to her and turned away.

She slipped her arms into it, still staring blankly at him.

"Ramsay—" Her voice was quiet and patient. "My dear, what *is* the matter with you? *Why* have you called the police? Please tell me what on earth is . . ."

He turned from the door into the inner hall that he had opened to turn on the light out there. It had been locked too, but he did not want to think of that now either. He turned and looked at her standing there, her blonde hair neatly secured in a silk net, all the make-up gone from her face, faintly shiny with night cream. A sudden awful compassion dissolved all the frozen agony inside him.

"Andrea, did you . . . hear anything, outside?"

He knew he was hesitating between the words, trying to choose them. But his speech always stumbled when he was overwrought, and she could take its meaning the way she wished.

"Hear anything outside?" She was so patiently bewildered that for one moment Ramsay Huse-Lorne clutched at a desperate hope. Then she raised her brows with a faint smile. "I heard you come barging in and knock the chair against the table in the hall. I was reading, waiting for you to get in. That's all I heard. I went to sleep after that. But I still don't know why you've called the police . . . ?"

"I called them because there's a man's body in the cistern."

He said it quietly. Something seemed to happen in his throat, paralyzing any further sound, and in his vision, fogging his glasses so that the image of her standing there, in horror-struck incredulity, seemed oddly blurred and not very real. But her instant reaction from what he'd said was real.

"You must be crazy as well as drunk . . ."

The brutal edge of her voice suddenly coarsened as the sound of a double knock on the front door came through the silent house. She yanked the belt of her dressing gown around her and tied it.

"And don't stand there like a gawking fool. You called the police, go and let them in. They'll think you've lost your mind. And if anybody has fallen into the cistern, it's your own fault. I've begged you a million times to padlock the thing."

Her eyes blazed contemptuously at him. "You and your

silly rock garden. You and your fancy drains. Go let them in before they wake the entire street. Or do I have to do it?"

She flashed past him, brushing the blue, silk net off her head with a swift thrust of her hand, rumpling her smooth hair, leaving him standing in the open doorway, stupefied by the venomous virulence of her attack. He put his dazed hand to his glasses and rubbed them up and down the bridge of his nose. Her slippers were still on the floor beside her bed. She was out there barefooted. His mind, struggling up out of a profound abyss, seemed to seek release in some ridiculous minutia. He moved over and bent down to get the blue slippers, and picked them up, lifting the trailing edge of the silk blanket cover as he did. His red hairy hand stopped and he let go the slippers. Behind them, he saw the toe of another soiled sneaker. The sole was still damp, and a damp blade of grass was stuck in the curving welt where the rubber turned up along the canvas top. He dropped it and moved back sharply, his face turned toward the hall as he listened to her releasing the chain on the front door and opening it for the men outside.

"Oh, Colonel . . . I'm so glad you've come!"

He heard the relieved anxiety in her voice, not believing it could be hers.

"Something dreadful must have happened. Ramsay thinks someone has fallen into the cistern in the garden. Come this way. Through my room. I'll turn on the flood light. Down on the lower terrace. You know, where Ramsay's rock garden is. I've got to put on some shoes."

He heard the deep, sympathetic murmur of Colonel Renfrew's voice, and the heavy steps drowning the flat patter of her bare feet coming along the hall. He looked down quickly. The shiny rubber sole of one shoe stuck out from under the silk blanket cover that had caught when he dropped it. He acted without stopping to think of the meaning of what he did. When the police came through the room, the shoe was hidden, Major Huse-Lorne was on the veranda.

The click of the switch under his hand flooded the garden with white brilliant light, all the shadowy forms and looming mystery of the night diminishing abruptly into the starkly-drawn commonplace. His eyes traveled slowly over it. He hated the place. He was curiously aware that he had always hated it . . . the dry, static artificiality of it, all made, all forced, never dead but always dying, nothing natural, all the

84

sub-tropical glamour of it put in and pulled out of the barren, bitter soil always washing out of the crevices of the unfriendly rock. It was evil. There was a brooding malice over it, over all the island, puny and rock-ribbed, as narrow as the souls of the . . .

"Are you coming, darling? Or are you still too upset?"

Huse-Lorne was aware of Colonel Renfrew turning at the top of the stairs to shoot him a curious, surprised glance.

"I'm just stopping to see if the light is going to be all right," he said calmly. "It's not been used since the hurricane last fall. I expect it's all right."

He followed them down. Colonel Renfrew was still trying to dissuade Andrea from coming. "No place for a lady, you know."

No place for a lady. It beat a monotonous threnody in Huse-Lorne's mind as he followed them. Andrea had put on the rubber-soled sneakers again.

12

The hard, white glare of the floodlight coming through the tilted slats of the venetian blinds threw their shadows horizontally on the opposite walls and along the bed. It was like being in a barred cell. For an instant the illusion held Betsy there, sitting up, half-awake, listening intently to the sound of voices and of moving feet on the iron stairs. Their presence there, the firm business-like tread of their feet coming closer as she listened, had a meaning too clear for her to refuse any longer to recognize it. She pushed the sheet back once more and got up, putting on her slippers and dressing gown, her breath coming quickly as she heard them then just outside the cottage, going down the rock stairs along the side of it to the lower terrace. She could see the square hole built in the flagstones down there, as she and Major Huse-Lorne had stood over it, peering down into the black cavern, black and glistening as oily pitch where the light caught the surface of the water.

He had dropped a pebble from the terrace into it, making a hollow, dull sound as the ripples coiled silently off and disappeared.

"Corking good place for The Body, what?"

She could hear him laughing delightedly as he said it, and shivered, remembering she had laughed too. But . . . if something had happened down there . . . whose body? And whose hand? Two people had gone down the stone steps before she heard the splash. The fact that no one had cried out, there had been no alarm, or any sound, was what had made her believe it was really only a coconut splashing in the pool, the sound magnified by the silence of the night and her own acute nervousness. Whose hand? Whose silent lips?

Her eyes moved with a kind of fascinated horror over to the small bottle of aspirin tablets on her bedside table. She thought of her father again. Death seemed to creep in all around her, silent and insidious. At least she had been warned, twice—three times, even—she thought, shuddering a little. She glanced over to the window, listening to the subdued voices coming up from the terrace.

Go out. Go out and see what's happened. Don't just keep standing here. She made herself turn and start across the room to the front door, aware that she had to make herself do it. She didn't want to go. She wanted not to go. *I'm being crazy. I just don't want to believe it, any of it. I just don't want to believe that anyone wants to . . .* She stopped there, still shrinking from the idea that she, Betsy Dayton, was actually and really in danger. It was all so preposterous. Even if it were so, it was still some kind of a mistake . . . a mistake that had all come about because *they* thought she had knowledge she didn't have, and had come to Nassau for a purpose that had never remotely been in her mind. Suddenly, her hand on the key in the lock, already moving to turn it, a flash of understanding struck her, stating the truth literally and clearly for the first time.

This is it. This is the knowledge. She did have it, now. The knowledge that her father had been murdered . . . that Miss Gurney had been murdered. That was what they thought she knew. It was like having gone up one flight of fantastic stairs and being so stunned by what she found there that she hadn't seen the second flight to another floor, where the sharper, clearer truth was lying in wait for her. Of course. They thought she knew, so they had to kill her. And if they knew now that Henry had warned her . . .

Instantly something inside her snapped together. She put her hand up to the switch by the door and clicked it sharply down. The lights in the room went on, dissolving all the shadows. The bars fell from her mind as they fell from the window and the walls. She went quickly back across the room to the table by her bed, took the bottle of tablets and put it in her pocket, looking around her, aware that if she had turned on the light before, instead of creeping through the eerie shadows, burdened with non-existent bars, she would have made sense sooner. She ran to the door, turned the key and opened it. She had no intention of being killed, not in Nassau or any place else, and not by Charles Cavanaugh, either by himself or anybody he'd hide behind. Her resentment rose in white-hot anger as she stepped out onto the narrow porch. *They . . .* she thought bitterly. She'd said *They* because that was what Henry had written, but she knew it was only a disguise in his mind as it was in her own.

The Beckwiths' lights were on. She saw them across the high pink wall and stood there, her hand on the porch rail, listening expectantly. Someone was coming. She could hear swift steps. Perhaps it was Scott. Her heart gave a quick, panicky leap in spite of all her resolution, and her knees began to shake as she found herself hoping, almost agonizingly hoping, it would be him.

"Scott!"

She saw him through the gate and ran blindly down the steps to the patio. If he'd just put his arms around her for one second . . . Then her feet froze to an abrupt halt. Charles Cavanaugh was coming through the gate behind him.

"Betsy! Are you okay? What the hell's going on here?"

She heard him, but her eyes going past him to his uncle did not see his arms go out toward her, or read the anxiety and desire in his face. All she saw was Charles Cavanaugh. Scott's arms dropped to his side. He looked at her, and back at his uncle. The same pattern still. If he had been able to find Charles Cavanaugh before he'd got home and gone to bed, he might have been a little closer to some kind of explanation.

"What's happened here, Betsy?"

It was Charles Cavanaugh's cool deep voice asking that.

"I don't know. Something back there. I was just going to see."

Cool herself. Cool as all get out. Scott watched her shuttered face, as expressionless as the wall behind her as she turned and went quickly on ahead of them. He looked back again at his uncle. It was just as curious that Charles, who'd been the one who waked him, so all-fired anxious for them to come over and see what was up, seemed now suddenly to have lost interest, quite indifferent about the whole thing, as if no matter what it turned out to be, his anxiety was already quite dispelled.

Until they got almost to the bottom of the steps to the lower terrace . . . Scott saw the white-topped yachting cap in the hands of one of the policemen there, before he saw the drenched inert figure lying on the flagstones. Henry lay on his stomach, his face turned to one side as a police attendant kneeling above him, his hands grasping the wizened body, smaller even than Scott remembered, forced the water out of his lungs, trying to force life back. He was already shaking his head.

"He's gone, sir," he said. He put a hand forward and lifted the sparse stringy wet hair above the temple. The bruised flesh was pulpy-soft under the pressure of the finger he laid on it. He shook his head again.

Scott, still on the bottom step, had not realized until then that he had taken Betsy's arm, and that the tremor he had felt shuddering through it at first had stopped. Her body was quiet and taut, pressed back against the rock wall of the steps, her eyes distended with a kind of inner horror that seemed to build up a rock wall of its own around her. He was aware then that Charles Cavanaugh, who had been behind the two of them, had thrust roughly past and was going across the flagstones. He could not see his face, but he saw the knot of men there fall back, an involuntary movement as significant as the simple gesture of the man holding Henry's cap. He held it out to Charles Cavanaugh, who took it silently and stood for a moment, his heavy shoulders rigid there in the white light, by the little man's side. He knelt down on one knee, turned the body over, looking down at the sharp ferrety face, his hand grasping the thin shoulder in its drenched blue flannel jacket.

"Henry . . ."

He shook the body a little, as if Henry would hear him and answer, get up and go along—as he might have shaken him if he had simply passed out in some dingy barroom on the waterfront.

"I'm afraid he's done for, sir." The man in the military uniform with the colonel's pips spoke.

Charles Cavanaugh glanced up.

"I realize it," he said curtly. "What is presumed to have happened to him?"

Scott was aware of the others there, beside Charles Cavanaugh kneeling by the little man's body and Betsy still enclosed in her own rigid wall. Andrea Huse-Lorne's bright inquiring blue eyes seemed to be fixed on Cavanaugh. There was no expression of pity or compassion on her set face. It was her husband who seemed moved, even profoundly moved, as if by some deep shock. Scott looked curiously at him. It was strange that such a drooping, cow-like apathy could be so revealing of human emotion as his was. Major Huse-Lorne seemed to feel an almost horror-stricken responsibility to Charles Cavanaugh personally, from the way his face contracted, as if a spasm of pain had shot through it, and he turned from Cavanaugh as if ashamed to have to face him there over the inert body.

"What is presumed to have happened to him?"

Charles Cavanaugh's question, bitterly edged under his curt even tone, seemed to create an abrupt tension. It was surprise, more than anything else, perhaps, Scott thought. He saw the police faces drop into expressionless official blanks, eyes shifting in military unison to the colonel standing by Huse-Lorne.

"I don't believe there's much doubt about what happened, sir," Colonel Renfrew said quietly. "These are private grounds. He seems to have got in here in some way, tripped and fallen into the cistern. I understand he is your pilot, in your employ. It's understandable you should be perturbed. But the Huse-Lornes have equal reason to be perturbed at trespassers in the middle of the night. They're both exceedingly distressed. However, if you are not satisfied it was an accident, we'll make a further investigation tomorrow, when we can see better what happened. Find out who's responsible for the cistern being left uncovered—if it was left uncovered."

He signed to the men by the narrow stretcher leaning against the stone wall. They came forward with it and halted, waiting for Cavanaugh to move aside. He stayed there, motionless. For an instant Scott tensed, a sharp warning ringing in his mind, quick chills racing up and down his spine. If Charles Cavanaugh refused to move, if he let himself go then, there was going to be plenty of trouble. He saw the suffused passion darkening the bland lineless face, the cords harden and bulge, the veins swelling, on his uncle's powerful neck, his jaws clamping coldly together. He was like a pit bull poised there savagely. Then, as swiftly and subtly as his passionate fury had coiled and spiraled, it faded out, and Charles Cavanaugh rose and moved quietly aside.

"I would appreciate an investigation," he said coldly.

"Very good, Mr. Cavanaugh."

One of the men had taken a notebook out of his tunic pocket.

"His name, please, sir?"

Charles Cavanaugh turned his head slowly, looking at him, his jaw hardening again. Scott moved uneasily. It was strange for Charles to have his anger roused a second time by a simple necessary question that he was the obvious person to expect an answer from.

"His name?" Charles Cavanaugh said slowly. "His name was Henry Grantson."

"Next of kin?"

"He has no kin that I am aware of. He had a daughter, I believe. It is my understanding that she died a good many years ago."

He turned on his heel and crossed the terrace. At the foot of the steps he turned back. "You may send me the notification of his death. So far as I know he had neither relatives nor friends."

He passed Scott and Betsy silently and went on up the stairs.

"We'll look into it in the morning," Colonel Renfrew repeated. "I must say, however, it does look fairly obvious," he added patiently.

Scott followed his glance across the wet flagstones to the dark line that marked the shadow of the wall. A broken whiskey bottle lay in a small wet pool, as if it had been thrown there—as it would have fallen if thrown by someone stumbling at the top of the cistern and dropping it as he tried to catch himself.

"We'll leave things as they are, please, Ramsay. Except the cover. I expect we'd best put that back on, if you'll give me a hand."

They lifted the cover back into place. It was not heavy. Scott looked at it. Not quite flush with the cut stone around it. Still, if it had been on . . . He shook his head. Henry had not always been too steady on his underpinning. He did have a bad leg, to boot.

Colonel Renfrew turned to Betsy.

"Major Huse-Lorne tells me you're staying in his cottage, Miss Dayton."

Scott felt her stiffen as if to prepare herself.

"I'm wondering if you heard any . . . well, any unusual noise or commotion, out here? Your windows are close, of course?"

Scott waited for her to speak. As she hesitated, he had the odd impression, for a moment, that they were all waiting for her, especially Huse-Lorne, who still seemed strangely distressed by all of it. His eyes met Mrs. Huse-Lorne's for an instant. She shook her head a little. "It's all too bad, I'm sorry," she seemed to be saying.

"You may have heard something without realizing what it was, at the time?"

"No," Betsy said. "I'm sorry . . . You see, I just got here today. I was very tired, and there are so many strange noises. I'm afraid I didn't hear anything at all."

"That's a blessing," Major Huse-Lorne said. He spoke gravely. It sounded curiously as if he meant it, not just as a manner of speaking, and that he would have been even more distressed if she had had that to remember along with the rest of it. Scott Beckwith looked at him, over there between his wife and the police officer. You would not have thought a long, drooping sort of cow-like face like his could show so much genuine feeling, or that the kind of bumbling, stuttering person he had appeared to be earlier that day would be actually moved by just one little no-good Cockney getting it like that.

"If there'd been any kind of row, she'd have heard it, I should think. Don't you, Ramsay?"

Mrs. Huse-Lorne's voice was as bright and brittle as usual.

"I don't know, I'm sure."

"Well, that's all down here, then."

Colonel Renfrew looked at Andrea, waiting for her to go past them. She came quickly over and put her hand on Betsy's arm.

"Come along, dear," she said. "Perhaps a good stiff drink would help all of us. Let's go to the house. Will you come, Scott?"

"No, thanks. I don't think I want a drink right now."

He followed her and Betsy up the stairs. Huse-Lorne and Renfrew stayed a moment. He heard them behind him, one pair of steps brisk and determined, the other slow and heavy as if weighted with lead.

"Would you like to come up to the house and stay tonight?" Mrs. Huse-Lorne said. "Or shall I come in and sit a while? But you have Scott, don't you." She smiled and patted Betsy's shoulder. "See that she's safely inside, Scott. Mr. Cavanaugh has got me nervous too. I think I'll go take an aspirin or something."

Her husband and Renfrew were up the stairs. She went with them across the garden. Betsy turned and hurried the few steps to the porch of the cottage. Her face, set and white, lingered for a moment as an after-image of extraordinary vividness on Scott's retina as the floodlight went abruptly off and the garden was instantly pitch-black.

13

Her face emerged, a pale quiescent oval, as his eyes became used to the dark again and the luminous starlight slowly re-created the looming shadowy forms of the vines, the cottage, the wall, and the gate in the wall, with the soft light from their own porch making a broad, filmy haze across the garden. The crabgrass looked like a gray-green carpet. He saw his uncle moving across it, moving forward and back, pacing the lawn slowly, like a caged animal. It was not often he felt any strong sense of kinship or sympathy with Charles Cavanaugh, but he did then. He had never thought of what Charles thought about Henry, or Henry about him. It was just one of those relationships, frequently irritating to the Beckwiths but apparently satisfactory to the two of them. Henry had not been a servant exactly; more like a retainer who functioned in whatever capacity the circumstances called for. When he was on tap, that is. Half the time when the Beckwiths would have liked him to be there to look after Charles, he was off somewhere, heaven only knew where. Then he'd turn up, the mixture as before. Charles must have had a kind of affection for him, difficult as it was to imagine between the two of them. But as he saw the light slanting across his uncle's thick shoulders, he realized he had himself had a sort of affection for the rat-faced little man, and a good deal for Charles Cavanaugh.

"Stay here a second, will you, Betsy?" he said. "I'll be back."

He forgot for the moment that she did not think so much of Uncle Charles. He was thinking about her in other terms, none of them clearly defined, all mixed up in a general apprehensiveness he had to settle, somehow, before he went back to bed. But he had to speak to Charles.

"You wait here a minute, will you, Betsy?"

He went across through the gate. Charles had left the terrace. He looked around for him. He hadn't gone into the house. It still had the silent, deserted look a house has with the lights on and no one up in it. His parents' room was dark. He smiled without amusement. His mother was up there, probably, eaten alive with curiosity but bound by the rigid conviction that what went on next door was next door's business. Then he saw a flicker of light go on and off down the steps to the lower level. Charles was there, sitting on the side of the chaise longue, his shoulders hunched forward, a cigarette in his hand, staring down at it. He glanced up briefly as Scott came down.

"What do you want?"

His voice was hard-edged. Scott hesitated. It was hard to put it into words. Nothing could be clearer than that Charles Cavanaugh did not want his sympathy.

"If you've come down to mewl over Henry, you can get out. He asked for it, he got it. He can't complain, blast his sniveling soul to hell."

Scott stood at the bottom of the steps, startled by the savage brutality of the words. Cavanaugh turned slowly and looked at him, his face, normally as bland as a summer evening, convulsed with passion. "The——"

Scott thought he had heard men curse, but he knew then he had not. Quietly, his voice hardly audible as far as the steps, Charles Cavanaugh poured out a stream of molten words that was unbelievable to him, its violence and hideous bitterness so intense that he would have said it was as if something Charles had wanted desperately, planned on, needed desperately to have, had been torn from him by the little man's infernal will to death.

Abruptly Charles Cavanaugh stopped. He stood up, went across the stone pavement to the low wall looking down on the quietly shining roofs of the little town under the hill, stood there a long time, it seemed to Scott, and turned back.

"That girl," he said curtly. His voice still shook with the dregs of passion not yet spent. "I want to talk to her."

A dangerous light flickered in Scott's eyes. He was a Beckwith then, no Cavanaugh.

"Not tonight," he said deliberately. "She's had a lousy enough time of it already, thanks to . . ."

"She'll have a lousier one before she's through this business."

The brutal edge was back on Cavanaugh's voice again.

"Find out what she's down here for. Watch her."

He started across the terrace to the other stairs going up.

94

Halfway there he turned. "Or if you're fool enough to be in love with her, get her out of here and keep her out. She's no good here."

He strode on to the steps and up them. Scott looked after him, watching him till he disappeared. This was a new Charles Cavanaugh. He could have counted half a dozen before that, and several of them he did not want to count, or even think about, but this was a complete stranger, from the sound of his voice to the livid fury distorting his face. A sudden flash of alarm shot through Scott's mind as he stood there.

"The guy's nuts. He's cracked."

It was what his mother was always worried might happen, and it looked as if it had happened. There was no other way to explain it. He ran back up the stairs. It was frightening. There was no telling what he might do. "That girl . . . watch her." It had sounded like a savage threat. It sounded so still as he recalled it. He ran across the lawn to the gate.

"Betsy!"

"Here I am."

The small, quiet sound of her voice sank into the taut fabric of his disturbed mind. He slowed down, more relieved than he could admit. He saw her then, huddled on the cottage steps, her arms folded around her drawn-up knees, her hands stuck into the sleeves of her coat. She looked like a small, lonely waif somebody had abandoned on a doorstep. For a moment the tenderness that swelled his heart was too overwhelming for him to think, much less to speak. He came over and sat down on the step beside her, and sat there a long moment before he took her hands from their small, tight huddle in her sleeves and held them.

"You know I love you, don't you, Betsy," he said. "I love you very much."

Moonlight and palms, the soft, caressing fingers of the sub-tropical zephyrs whispering through feathery pines . . . that was the way he had thought of it, back in Chicago. Betsy in something long and white and filmy beside him . . . not huddled up in a wrinkled pajama suit, her face a white blob, no lipstick, her hair like a very clean rat's nest, no moonlight, just a few milky-looking stars pushed aside by the light through the iron gate across the crab grass from their porch, and another one upstairs at the Huse-Lornes', and himself not much to offer just then, forgetting all the ways he had planned to say it, masterful or tenderly casual, depending on

95

the mood of the enchanted moment. It wasn't the way he had intended it to be.

"You do know, don't you, Betsy?"

He kissed her cheek softly. She trembled a little and turned her dark eyes toward him.

"Do you? I wasn't sure. I . . . I'm very glad."

"You're sure now, Betsy. And I want you to be glad."

They sat there soberly. *Where was the moonlight, and the grand passion of her lips straining to his?* It was not the way he had pictured it, but it was so profoundly and miraculously moving to him, sitting there, that he didn't want it any different just then.

"You're going to marry me, Betsy. Right away. As soon as——"

He could see her shaking her head slowly. "No."

"Why not?"

"Because . . . I can't." She had no idea at all of how to say it to him. She might just as well say it the way it was. "Because somebody must . . . somebody is trying to kill me. Actually to——"

He heard the words, but with the entranced lightness of his heart and the miraculous fog that hovered like a bright cloud around her head, they had no real meaning.

"Look, Betsy," he said gently. "Uncle Charles has some-how got you all upset. He's given everybody the jitters. But . . . we mustn't be psychotic about it, Betsy. Henry must have been drunk and fallen in there. You saw the whiskey bottle. He drank too much sometimes. He was probably trying to get up to our place next door and got here instead."

"That isn't true, Scott."

She hesitated again, and went on steadily.

"He didn't make a mistake. He came here because I was here. And he wasn't alone. Not when he went down there. Somebody was with him. I . . . I didn't tell the truth when they asked me. I did hear them. And Henry was pushed into the cistern because he was trying to warn me. I . . . I know it."

She fished in her pajama pocket and took out the bottle of tablets, holding it out toward him. He recognized the famil-iar shape and label without having to see it distinctly.

"It's my aspirin bottle—the one I got at the air field. It was in my dressing case. I got up to take one because my head was aching and I couldn't go to sleep. I came back in my room to get some water out of the thermos bottle. That's when I heard them outside—and then I saw the note there under the door. It said not to take any pills, because that . . . that was the way they killed my father."

He listened silently, not moving.

"That's why I . . . I know somebody is trying to kill me too. Because I looked, just now, while you were gone. The tablets are all labeled, you know. But one of these isn't. One at the top. It's almost the same size, but it's plain, it's not labeled. And it was a new bottle, and I can tell the wad of cotton has been pulled out. That's not all. Henry tried to warn me, this afternoon, on the boat. That's why he backed it offshore, not to scare me but to warn me to get out and go home. He said I wasn't safe. And I . . . I couldn't think how he could know anything at all about me . . . even who I was, or anything. But I think now I know how he knew."

She sat there for a long moment without speaking, reaching back into a dimly-remembered past that was slowly taking form, becoming real and living and more sharply distinct in her mind.

"I'd forgotten until just a minute ago, when I looked at the tablets to see if they were . . . all right. Then I remembered, all of a sudden. Henry's name was Grantson. When your Uncle Charles said that was it, down there, I . . . I sort of knew I'd heard it before, but I couldn't think where. Then it came to me. The other girl in the office, the one who disappeared after the fire . . . Her name was Harriet Grantson. She must have been——"

"My dear children . . . aren't you ever going to bed?"

Both of them, close to each other there on the steps, started violently. They got quickly to their feet. Andrea Huse-Lorne was hardly five feet from them. She was still in her tailored blue satin robe, wide awake and smiling. She was close enough for them to see her red lips and her white teeth glistening.

"I thought I heard someone down here, and I didn't want my poor Betsy frightened out of her wits. I'm glad it's only you, Scott. But I do think you ought to go home and let Betsy go to bed. Ramsay has terribly old-fashioned ideas."

Mrs. Huse-Lorne laughed, shrugging her shoulders lightly. "So do run along, Scott. You can see the child in the morning. Good night, Betsy. I'll send you some coffee at nine."

14

Mrs. Huse-Lorne went back to the house and up the wrought-iron stairs to the balcony. She waited there until the lights in the cottage went off, and again for a moment until the light filtering through the gate from the Beckwiths' house went off too. It left her own light shining palely out, meeting and merging softly with the luminous starlight, the only visible sign of wakefulness in the long and now silent night. Ramsay's room was dark, but she knew he was not asleep, and she moved quietly, but without stealth, ready for him if he should come shambling out there again. "Just sending that silly boy home, darling, so Betsy can get to bed." It was ready on the tip of her tongue, but he did not come out. A frail wisp of something that might have been a warning if she had stopped to analyze it stirred in the back of her mind. He was always so hoveringly solicitous about her that it seemed strange, now, for him to let her wander about without bumbling out to see if he could get anything or do anything for her. Or it would have been strange to her if she had thought about it instead of brushing it off, glad that for once he had sense enough to leave her alone. Not sense. It wasn't that she had to thank. It was his squeamish belly. You'd think he'd never seen anybody dead before, in spite of two wars, and just because it happened in his own back yard.

She waited a moment longer, watching the iron gate in the wall to see that Scott Beckwith did not come slipping back. Maybe it had been a mistake to open it up, after all . . . and she was at the point now where she could not afford to make mistakes of any kind. She had to stop now and think seriously and to definite purpose. That was why she wanted to be sure all of them had gone to bed, as if, somehow, their being awake and close to her would be in itself a form of communication she could not afford to risk.

She went across to the door and inside. She sat down on the side of her bed, took off the rubber-soled shoes, held them knee high and dropped them onto the floor before she got into bed and switched off the light. Then she waited a moment before she drew her body cautiously and silently up into a sitting position, and sat there, her mind drawing itself into sharp concentration, her peripheral senses still alert for any sound or change in the eerie luminescence outside her door. It was time to take stock, to evaluate the things that had happened. The fact that the hands lying tense on the cool smooth surface of the blue silk blanket cover were heavy with a calmly calculated, cold-blooded murder had no special meaning to her, at this point. Henry Grantson. Harriet Grantson. They were names she could repeat as if they were Smith, Jones or Robinson . . . part of so remote a past, the intervening time span so intensely more to her satisfaction, and so intensely vivid compared to the past they had been part of, that they might never have existed or been part of her own history. They were like whistle stops on the prairie. Her train had stopped there for a moment and gone on to a shining metropolis, and she would never have had to think of them again, if they had not gotten themselves uprooted and planted perversely in the way.

The one called Henry Grantson, that is. He had been so little a part of his daughter's life, half derelict, half wanderer, never contributing anything and mooching off her when he could . . . He ought to have been dead years ago, she thought coolly. How he had found Andrea Huse-Lorne, how he had recognized her, she still did not know. It was what she had planned to find out from the minute the galvanic shock of her own real half-forgotten name, and his, came over the telephone that evening, bringing for the first time a threat that she knew, when it came, she had always, in some profound way, been half-expecting and waiting for.

And ready for, Mrs. Huse-Lorne thought, her eyes contracting in the semi-darkness of her room. Blackmail. Her extraordinary ego could call it that, and had done so without an instant's hesitation. And without even that much hesitation she could arrange to meet him—anxiously, in fact. And perhaps if it had been simple blackmail, she could have let him off—let him off at least until she had found out how he had known who and where she was. But money he didn't want. Or so he'd said. She raised her brows, smiling derisively. It was the girl, he'd said. Betsy Dayton. He was going to warn her . . . or go to the police if anything should happen. The sneaking, treacherous, little fool hadn't admitted he'd already warned her. And she—stupidly, she could admit that to herself—had taken it for granted something had already happened to Betsy Dayton. The drawn, headachy look around the girl's eyes in the afternoon, the bottle of aspirin just on top of her dressing case, showing it was something she took naturally and normally enough to carry with her, wherever she went . . . her light when she had first gone to the cottage, going on and off, on and off, and the bathroom light going on and off, and then no more light down there . . . it had built up a progressive pantomime to her watching eye that seemed as plain as if she had seen her open the bottle, pour the white tablet into her hand, toss it into her mouth and pffft. An instant was all it took.

And so far from having any fear or panic at the hoarse threatening whisper out there, of the little man, spraying out his unclean saliva so she recoiled, revolted, from it, she had had a moment of almost exultant exhilaration. Henry Grantson and Elizabeth Dayton, both of them, the last shreds that tied her to the other buried life, the last weak shreds that might inexplicably weave themselves into a net to trap her unconscious feet, they were both there, one destroyed, the other a mere matter of cunning and tact, getting him down to the lower terrace where she had already taken the cover off the cistern, and that was that. He was too nervous, too jittery, and a little too retarded by the liquor she could smell on his breath that he must have filled himself with to screw up his courage to come to see her at all, to dare talk to her the way he had.

And the shock as she came back, seeing the light go on again in the cottage bathroom . . . The shock of finding that Ramsay was still mooning about that had been unimportant, compared with it. It was still unimportant. She dismissed him now with even less interest. Ramsay was a vacant, bumbling fool, half-blind even in the daytime. The small green snake of her contempt for him uncoiled itself in her heart and slithered away. But he was still useful. His calling the police was a stroke of luck, now she thought of it. Colonel Renfrew *knew* he was an honorable man. It was a good thing she had managed to keep her mouth shut, down there, difficult as it had been, the way Renfrew took for granted— like an Englishman—that it was Ramsay's house and Ramsay was the head of it. And Ramsay was an honorable man. Fine.

She dismissed Ramsay. To come back to Elizabeth Dayton . . . Her lips tightened to a thin cruel line. Her mistake had been to let herself be blinded by the fear and panic that had riddled her, with its stupefying deadliness, that morning. The way she had talked to Scott, just now at the cottage, it almost looked as if she hadn't known . . . until Henry Grantson had got to her. Henry Grantson. Harriet Grantson. Mrs. Huse-Lorne smiled slowly. Elizabeth Dayton had not remembered Harriet Grantson until Charles Cavanaugh had spoken the name of Harriet's father . . . and not even then . . . not until she'd found the unmarked tablet among the marked ones in her aspirin bottle. That was what Henry Grantson must have warned her about then . . . not about Harriet Grantson. Mrs. Huse-Lorne thought intently. So that now Elizabeth Dayton knew someone was trying to get rid of her. Someone . . . not Andrea Huse-Lorne. And nobody was left now to tell her, nobody left who could jog her childhood memory and bring back associations. Still, the train of them was started. Fear could be the propelling force moving it on of its own accord. The tablet in the bottle was a mistake—but, in the light of the aftermath, a mistake only because it had not worked. And there was no time for any more mistakes.

A worried line etched itself between her smooth brows. There was still Charles Cavanaugh. If Henry Grantson had talked to him . . . Mrs. Huse-Lorne shook her head. If he had, one thing was certain: Charles Cavanaugh would not have allowed Elizabeth Dayton to stay in the cottage. She closed her eyes and brought his face and figure back on the silent screen of her mind. No. He was nobody she knew, or had ever known or ever seen. Nobody like Charles Cavanaugh had ever come into the dreary, submerged life that Harriet Grantson had led. Perhaps if someone like him had . . . She brushed that aside—it was unimportant anyway—trying to remember precisely what Charles Cavanaugh had said to Andrea Huse-Lorne that afternoon, talking about Jerome Dayton. The live terror she had known then seemed to have blotted out of her mind all the nuances that she could now have looked back at to reassess. He had said an employee had disappeared. But that was casually, when Ramsay had butted in. And down on the terrace, he had said he believed she had been dead for some years. There was nothing to connect the two . . . nothing but the crawling, creeping, despicable fear in her own mind. And Henry Grantson . . . She could feel the specks of saliva on her cheek again as he spat the words at her, his sibilant passionate half-whisper, half-snarl, grating in her ears, evil-smelling in her nostrils.

"I've kept mum. W'y? Becos 'oo'd believe a bloke like me? Nobody. They'd s'y, 'e's off 'is rocker, the bloody bastid. 'E's not syfe to 'ave about. Lock 'im up! That's wot they'd s'y. That's wot they did s'y in New York when I tried to tell 'em. Shove me in the can all night to sober up, they said. So I shut me ruddy trap. But I won't keep it shut, I won't!"

"But I'm afraid you will, my dear." Andrea Huse-Lorne stirred with a cat-like contentment. Then she raised her head, listening intently. She thought she heard a sound from her husband's room. But she did not hear it again, and she moved silently out of her bed onto the floor. She crept softly over to her dressing room, took out the navy blue silk robe hanging inside the door, slipped it on, and put on a pair of thin-soled ballet slippers. She took the dark thin silk scarf out of the pocket of her robe and bound it around her blonde shining hair. She waited a moment, listening again, before she pulled out a drawer, and from the back of it, behind the neat rolls of the light stockings she wore every day, took out a black silk pair. The black stockings she kept for funerals of state, and there was only one of the last pair she had there now. The other was ripped, and over in the locked dresser drawer where she kept her jewelry, to stay there until she had an opportunity to destroy it. Then, very softly, she went back into her room and picked up off the floor the intricately carved ball of quartz lapis lazuli, flattened on one side, that made a door stopper against the sub-tropical winds in the hurricane season. She slipped it into the stocking and wrapped the end into a tight, knotted thong around her wrist.

A thin smile moved one corner of her mouth. Ramsay, always reading what he called thrillers—always some day, by Jove, going to write one; make a packet of money, you know —would long since have forgotten the lesson in home commando technique he'd bored one of her dinner parties with. And if anyone should happen to remember it, they'd think of him, not her. She would have preferred some subtler method, but time was pressing. It had worked on Henry Grantson, who was far more suspicious of her than Elizabeth Dayton would be when she tapped lightly at her door . . . too restless to sleep, needing another woman to talk to . . . Not at the front door but at the door inside that led into the little hall above the staircase down to the maid's room. If she was in the habit of moving around without any lights on, Mrs. Huse-Lorne thought coolly, then perhaps she would not turn one on at the sound of Andrea Huse-Lorne's voice speaking through the closed door. She thought quickly: she didn't have to speak through the closed door. She'd forgotten. When she'd let the maid go, she'd locked the door herself. The key was still there, on the servant's side. All she had to do was unlock it . . .

She went silently to her own door and slipped out onto the veranda, holding the door as she halted, listening with avid tightly coiled intensity toward her husband's door. It was not the sound there that had made her stop. It was the absence of sound. If he was properly asleep she would be able to hear his heavy, maddeningly long drawn-out breath before it broke into a sharp snore and held, before it started at the bottom and climbed up to break again. But she heard nothing, not even the toss and turn of his lank body on the old camp bed that an officer of Napoleon's Grand Armée was supposed to have used and that she wanted for her guest room and couldn't get. It was curious to think of his small truculences and stubborn resistance to her perfectly simple plans at a time like this, and his sudden occasional recalcitrance that she found more and more maddening as he grew older.

She stood there undecided for a moment, then let her door close silently. Pressing her body against the wall, she edged carefully along it, a dark shadowy figure against the unbroken masonry, as still as the death she carried clenched tightly in her hand. She felt the frame of the long window next to his door. There was a curtain hanging inside it—he wouldn't have louvres or venetian blinds, in Dorset they had curtains at the windows—and she stopped there and turned her head so she could look inside, past the curtain. It was not the first time she had done it, and she did it now keyed to a sharper pitch than she had ever been when she'd watch him unlock and open the ridiculous strong box in his bottom bureau drawer, anxiously counting the few worthless pounds he'd hoarded there. But she could not see him now. When she did, her shoulders stiffened suddenly. There was something wrong. He must be sick. He was there on the floor beside his bed. She turned, edging closer to the masonry, to see him better. Then she raised her hand and moved it across her eyes, staring with an utterly blank incredulity at him.

Ramsay Huse-Lorne was on his knees. She moved back

abruptly, almost tripping when her foot struck the thick edge of the grass rug. The fool, the poor half-witted fool. He was on his knees, saying his prayers. For the love of . . . Mrs. Huse-Lorne swallowed with a kind of breathless amazement, completely dumbfounded. What in heaven's name was he praying for at that time of night! She knew he used always to say his prayers at night. It was the way he'd been brought up, and nothing changed him. She had been brought up that way too, but she'd gotten over it. He never did. It was so ridiculous, seeing a grown man down on his . . .

Andrea Huse-Lorne stiffened abruptly. Her mind racing actively, she caught her breath, a cold spasm catching her heart as if a knife had been driven into it. She caught the handle of her door, wrenched it open and ran swiftly across into her dressing room. She tore the scarf from her hair, tore the dark dressing gown from her shoulders. What if he had seen her . . . ? He could easily not have been on his knees, he could have seen her creep down the stairs into the garden. She ripped the quartz lapis lazuli doorstop out of the stocking, her whole body livid with frozen gooseflesh, her nails tearing ladder into the stocking as she freed the silk threads from the carved interstices of the stone. Her hands shook so that she had to grip it carefully to keep from dropping it on the floor. For a frantic instant, the need to hide it where nobody would see it was so overwhelming that she tore open her stocking drawer and put it inside, thrusting the drawer shut. Then she gripped the closet door to steady herself, rubbing her hand over her wet forehead.

"If he'd seen me . . ." Her mouth was dry as ground-up bones. She made her way across the room to the chair in front of her dressing table and let herself down into it. What if he had seen her? What if she had gone down and come back without looking into his window first? She stared at the black stocking lying on the floor where she had dropped it. She had to get rid of it. She had to get rid of the other one, in her locked jewel drawer. But how? She had destroyed three human beings, but the simple problem of destroying one pair of black torn stockings that could easily destroy her seemed at the moment an almost insurmountable task.

15

As Betsy woke from dreamless forgetfulness, it was waking as she always waked, alive and fresh to another day. She heard the mockingbirds in the flowing vines, their song as radiant as the golden planes of sunlight filling the room, as crystal clear as the blue of the sky through the emerald tracery of the palm leaves. She closed her eyes and opened them again, her heart swelling with a golden radiance all its own. The memory of the night was back, but only the lovely part of it. It filled her too full of its glowing enchantment to leave any room just then for the nightmare of anxiety and fear out of which it had sprung. "Sweet are the uses of adversity," she remembered suddenly.

> "Which, like the toad, ugly and venomous,
> Wears yet a precious jewel in his head."

She sat up and stretched her arms out, breathing deeply, profoundly happy. She dropped them at the light tap on the door from the servants' staircase, and the sound of a soft voice.

"Miss Betsy? It's Rose, Miss."

The key turned in the lock. No echo to tell her how it might have turned, and might have opened, in that dark moment that now was gone.

The Beckwiths' maid came in. "Good morning, Miss. It's a lovely day."

Her voice was as gently sweet as her smile. Betsy saw the quiet, fluid gracefulness of her hands as she set the breakfast tray over her lap. Tucked in one side of it was a single great yellow bloom, and inside it a folded slip of paper.

Rose smiled again and went softly out of the room as Betsy picked the paper up, her eyes shining as she read it.

"Betsy dearest— They call this a chalice flower. The Spaniards call it Copa del Oro. It's full of my love. You're never to forget it any more, Betsy. I love you very much. Scott."

105

She held the great golden cup in both her hands and raised it, her head bending to touch the waxen petals softly with her lips. *How sweet of him . . . how very sweet.*

Then Rose came back. "I'm sorry to disturb you, Miss," she said gently. "But Mr. Scott told me to remind you the men would be here to see about what happened. They've come. They're down there now. He said he would come over in half an hour, if you'd like to be ready, Miss. Then he said after that you'd go over to the Island. Would you like me to put the flower in some water, Miss?"

"Please." Betsy held it out, and the maid took it, almost sadly, as if she knew she was taking from her the first tangible symbol of her happiness, and leaving her hands suddenly empty, forcing her to forget that, and remember the other, darker, aspect of the morning.

"Thanks, Rose," she said. "Tell him I'll be ready."

She poured out a cup of coffee and picked up her glass of orange juice, her eyes following the girl as she came back from the bathroom and set the chalice flower in a crystal holder on the table beside her.

"I'm afraid there may be ants still on it, Miss."

Betsy's light, involuntary laugh broke a little. The tears came suddenly out along her lids. "That's all right," she said. "I'm afraid there's always something."

If ants were the only things she had to worry about, it would be wonderful. Ants you could brush off. If she could only brush off the rest of it as easily . . . But Henry's note couldn't be brushed off, or the tablet in the bottle of aspirin that Scott had taken with him last night. Or the murder of her father and Miss Gurney, and now of the little man who had lost his own life trying to save hers. And what to do? What to say to the police when they questioned her again this morning?

She turned her head, listening outside the window. She could hear them on the terrace, and hear Rose, closing the screen door as she went out of the maid's room and up the stone stairs by the cottage. The girl walked softly, but she could still hear her footsteps. Last night, she had heard Henry's and someone else's, lighter than his, she thought, as re-creating the image of the sound in her memory she re-called now the broken beat of his step, and the other one. She tried to bring the sound of the other one back more clearly, but it had been too dimly heard. She did recall another picture that had been lying just off in the background of her mind, and her heart sank a little as she thought of it. It was Charles Cavanaugh coming down the stairs at the Beckwiths', just before lunch. She could feel the tension in the two Beckwiths again, and see Charles Cavanaugh's feet on the steps as he came down, lightly, with the quick soft tread of the athlete. He had been wearing rope-soled shoes.

She pushed the idea quickly out of her mind. If only she had had more time to talk to Scott, before Mrs. Huse-Lorne had broken in on them, sending them both to bed. She wondered then, for the first time, how much Mrs. Huse-Lorne had heard of what she did say to him. They were talking very quietly, but sound was funny at night. If Mrs. Huse-Lorne had heard very much, or indeed almost anything, of it, she'd think it was odd if Betsy went on telling the police she'd seen nothing, heard nothing and knew still less. On the other hand . . . She swallowed the last drop of coffee and ate the rest of her toast. She was certainly a lot safer if she kept her mouth firmly shut—at least until she knew exactly what she was talking about. And if Andrea Huse-Lorne had heard her, she would tell the police. Or she'd tell her husband, and he'd tell them.

She moved the tray to the foot of the bed and got up to take a shower. At least, she thought, she'd keep still until she'd had a chance to talk to Scott . . . if she had the chance, if Mrs. Huse-Lorne hadn't heard her and already talked herself. But as she looked at her image in the mirror as she brushed her teeth, her heart rose again. It wasn't nearly as bad as it had been the night before. The twin angels of light and love had driven the blinding devil of terror back where he belonged. The miasma of evil was gone. There was danger still, but it no longer crawled and crept in the lonely dark. She could even sing as she turned on the shower and stood under it.

> "Dance, gal, dance,
>   Sponga money easy come,
>   Sponga money never done."

Who said it was a sad song? Some day she'd have to find out what the rest of it was.

They were already there on the Huse-Lorne veranda outside the cool blue depths of the drawing room as Scott called her. She ran out to join him, nothing but a smile and a quick handclasp to confirm for each of them their own private cup

107

of gold. Charles Cavanaugh was not there; Mr. Beckwith had come instead. Betsy went along between the two of them, greatly relieved that it was him instead of his brother-in-law. It seemed to make it easier already. Colonel Renfrew and Captain Lawson of the C. I. D. were seated between the Huse-Lornes, Andrea with hat and gloves on, dressed for the street, her big green glasses shielding her eyes from the glare of the sun, frowning at her husband, fidgeting over a thread that had come loose from the hem of his khaki-colored shorts.

"I'm sorry my brother-in-law isn't able to be here," John Beckwith said. "He is not quite up to it, this morning, I'm afraid."

Betsy glanced at Scott. He shook his head a little and looked away.

"Well, I'm afraid we've not found anything to change our view," Colonel Renfrew said. "We've been through Grantson's things on the boat and impounded them. He's been living there in the cabin. There's no apparent evidence, there or elsewhere, that he had enemies of any kind. The post mortem showed he'd been drinking, though not enough to make anybody under normal circumstances what you'd call drunk. He was lame, of course. From what we can tell, he seems to have come up the rocks behind your place, Mr. Beckwith, and climbed over the wall where it goes down there at the end of the two gardens."

He turned to Betsy.

"You've not thought of anything, Miss Dayton . . . changed your mind, I mean, about hearing a disturbance?"

She shook her head. The idea that had occurred to her a moment before slipped out of her mind as his question brought her back to the sharper incidents of the night before. If Henry had been living on the boat, he'd probably moved his wooden chest with the rope handles aboard with him anyway. The foot of the stairs in the pavilion had just been a temporary storage spot.

"And you, Ramsay?"

"As I've told you, Peter. I heard a splash. It sounded rather too loud to be the casual sort of droppings about one hears at night."

Major Huse-Lorne spoke stiffly, without stumbling, his eyes fixed owlishly in front of him.

"I thought I should go have a look. I did so. The white-topped cap was lying on the flagstones and the cover of the cistern was off to one side. I trod on some broken glass. I had my torch with me, and I could see there was a man at the bottom there. I came back to the house and got on to you at once. I didn't know the poor chap, but I had seen him, as I told you, at the Carlton with Mr. Cavanaugh, earlier in the evening."

Colonel Renfrew turned to Andrea. She shook her head.

"I didn't hear a thing, not till my husband waked me and said he'd called you." She hesitated a moment, as if not quite sure how to put it. "Can't you tell by the injuries whether . . ."

Colonel Renfrew nodded.

"That's the problem, of course. The wound on the side of his head seems perfectly clear. There's blood on the edge of the stone coping of the cistern, where he struck himself when he pitched forward. The other injury, to the top of his head, was presumably caused by his striking it on the rock at the bottom of the cistern. In the absence of any other evidence, that seems to be the answer. It could be he was struck on the head with some object before he went into the cistern. I was hoping Mr. Cavanaugh would be here to give us information—if he has any. If he feels, I mean, that there's any reason to believe there was foul play."

He turned to John Beckwith.

"We'll come with you, if you don't mind. I should really like to talk to him again. Perhaps he's not too unwell to talk to me a moment."

John Beckwith nodded and got to his feet. Colonel Renfrew turned to Huse-Lorne. "Unless we have further information, I think we're cleaned up here, Ramsay. We're talking to the people he was with around the waterfront. Something may turn up. But so far as we can see, there's nothing left here to go farther with. Your people all swear up and down the top was on the cistern when they cleared, after cocktails. But of course they would. One of them may talk, however, and we'll hear it."

Ramsay Huse-Lorne had got to his feet. There was a look so pained and stricken on his long sun-reddened face that Renfrew put his hand out and touched his shoulder.

"Don't feel it's too much your fault, old chap."

Huse-Lorne stepped aside so that his hand dropped abruptly. "Right," he said. "I'll see to it it doesn't happen again. Thanks, all of you."

He turned and went into the house. John Scott Beckwith

and the two policemen moved along. Mrs. Huse-Lorne shook her head and moved her hands in a small gesture of helplessness as she smiled a little at Scott and Betsy.

"Ramsay feels things so horribly. It's beyond me. Of course, I'm sorry, and distressed, and all that, but heavens, I don't see how we can be responsible for everybody who breaks into our grounds. It isn't as if it weren't a terrific job . . . just getting in, I mean. I certainly hope it doesn't alarm you about staying in the cottage, Betsy."

She got briskly to her feet.

"Well, I've got to get along. I've got a Gymkhana meeting at Government House. What are you children going to do? Why don't you get your suits and have a swim with Ramsay?"

"Thanks, but we've got to get on," Scott said. He took Betsy's hand and pulled her up out of her chair. "We're going to the Island for the day."

Andrea Huse-Lorne walked across the garden with them as far as the steps to the gate out into the street.

"Well, goodbye—have a good time. I'll see you."

She opened the gate, smiling around at them as she closed it behind her. They went along to the cottage, neither of them looking back to see Major Huse-Lorne come out of his room, go along the veranda to his wife's room and go inside.

He stood there sick at heart, unbearably sick, with an inner stupefaction that showed imperfectly in the long, almost ludicrous droop of his straw-colored mustache and in the torturing agony of his unhappy eyes. It was several moments before he could bring himself to bend down and pick up off the floor the carved ball of quartz lapis lazuli, flattened on one side to hold the door against the wind when the hurricane season swept over the tiny seagirt island in the Caribbean.

16

"I don't know what to do either, Betsy," Scott Beckwith said gravely.

They were in the small cottage room, sitting on the bed, made up now into its daytime semblance of a smartly tailored couch along the wall. The door was open, a couple of small gray lizards playing on its sunlit blue tiles, a mockingbird perched on the iron railing as tame and friendly as if neither cats nor men existed in its universe of bursting song.

"I thought the way you did. I thought if she'd heard you, she'd have told the Colonel. But I don't see how she could have. We didn't hear her. I can't imagine any dame like that, if she did hear you, not bursting in with 'Tell me more!' Somebody like Mother would have pretended she didn't hear, but not Andrea. She doesn't have that good bringing up in the first place. But of course, the names wouldn't mean anything to her. Grantson—Henry *or* Harriet."

The note Betsy had found thrust under the door was lying between them on the glazed chintz cover of the sofa. Scott picked it up and read it for the tenth time.

"You see, we always thought—the police thought—he was planning to run off with the money that was there, ready for him to take on the plane. The money, and Miss Gurney." She had told him all of it, as they sat there. Her mind now moved around and around, trying to understand. "He had to have it in cash, because it was a South American deal and the European war was already on. Of course, if I'd been older I'd know more. Mother and my father's family always tried to make me believe it was a heart attack that killed him. That's what the papers said. I don't know what it was that put the doubt in my mind, that made me decide to look it up myself. It was when I was in New York once, when I was a senior in college. The Inspector I talked to tried to persuade me not to insist on seeing the record, but he had to show it to me. A lawyer who was a friend of the family talked to him. That's why, I guess."

She looked over at the dressing table drawer where the

111

letter from Mary Davis was. She still hadn't showed him that. What do you do? You can't just say to a man who's asked you a second time to marry him, "Sorry, but I think it's your uncle. I know it sounds crazy but what else can I think? Do you mind telling me where your uncle got all his money? And why is he so concerned about my reason for being here?"

"This Harriet Grantson, Betsy," Scott said slowly. "Who was she? Do you remember her? Could she have . . ."

"That's what I've been trying to think," she said quickly. "I just remember her sort of vaguely. She was awfully quiet and mousey, but not mouse-nesty like Miss Gurney, if you know what I mean. And she was a lot younger than Miss Gurney. I don't know. Age when you're ten is hard to tell, but if Miss Gurney was forty-five, then Harriet Grantson would have been around twenty-eight or thirty, I guess. Maybe not even that. She was much nicer than Miss Gurney. It's an awful thing . . . but you know, I remember thinking, when I read about the plane reservations for my father and Miss Gurney, that I wouldn't have been so surprised if it had been the other one. She wasn't any . . . any snappier, but she had something."

She looked away for a moment.

"And her office—it was a sort of cubbyhole really—was right next to the lab where the two chemists had their stinks and things. That was one of the things the police files pointed out—my father being in the chemical business had easy access to cyanide. But . . . it was true of Harriet too, I suppose. And it was she who went and got his prescription filled that day, so she had opportunity. And being the bookkeeper, of course she'd know about the money. I seem to remember Miss Gurney was pretty tough on her. Maybe she'd hated her for years."

She sat there looking back, trying to re-create the images lost with her childhood. Scott watched her, listening silently. It was tough on the poor kid, but it might dredge up something useful for them to go on. It was, so far, simply unsubstantial.

"You see, I used to be there a lot, because I broke my arm and there was nothing for me to do, and my father used to give me problems to do on the calculating machines. Mother was pretty social and civic, with bundles for all sorts of things, and ambulance corps, and learning to be a plane spotter. And my father wanted me to be a chemist—the not

112

having a son sort of thing. When I'd get too bored, he'd ship one of them, either Miss Gurney or Harriet, off for the day to take me to a movie, or some place."

She looked up, sudden laughter in her brown eyes. "Oh, and I'd forgotten. Harriet had a beau. Oh yes, he was a taxi driver. He used to . . ."

The smile went out of her face with the suddenness of a light turned off against a blank wall. She put her hand up to her mouth, as if appalled at what had come into her mind and she'd been about to say.

Scott looked at her silently for an instant, waiting. Then he said, "What is it, Betsy?" He spoke very quietly, not to disturb the memory dawning in her mind.

"Nothing. It . . . it's nothing at all."

He got up and put his arms around her. She was trembling.

"Betsy, what is it? Tell me what you were thinking."

As she looked up at him a kind of desperate urgency widened her eyes. "Scott," she whispered. "I . . . I did remember something. This sounds utterly . . . utterly crazy. But I've got to ask you. Did your Uncle Charles ever drive a taxi?"

He drew a deep breath of relief.

"Uncle Charles . . . *drive a taxi?*" He dropped his arms to his sides, laughing a little. "Good grief, no. Look, my sweet . . . of course Charles never drove a taxi. What would Charles Cavanaugh be doing, driving a cab? He may be nuts now, but he hasn't always been. Charles Cavanaugh, my dear, whatever else he's been, has always been extremely well-heeled. He made most of it himself, and he never made it doing anything as useful as driving a cab, or digging a ditch, or even in the heavyweight ring. Charles is strictly amateur except at high-powered finance, and he pulls strings. He doesn't mine the copper or grease the works that pump the oil. Charles is strictly clean hands and white collar."

She looked at him intently, breathing evenly again, not trembling any more.

"Why did you ask that?"

She pushed the hair back from her forehead, smiling uncertainly. "I knew it sounded crazy. But I . . ."

She hesitated again. The thought persisted, the image gathered in less misty form in her memory.

"Go on, Betsy. You what? Look . . . you can't hurt my feelings about Charles. Look at him now. Straight down the old escape hatch. The minute anything goes wrong, or some-

113

thing happens our Charles doesn't like, off he goes."

She looked at him, not understanding. She had thought she knew what the matter was when John Beckwith had said he wasn't up to coming over. But when he took Colonel Renfrew and Captain Lawson to the house to see him . . .

Scott smiled a little unhappily at her. "Look, Betsy. You might just as well get the hang of this right now, because you're going to marry me, as soon as we get the dope on what the local ground rules are. So hush, honey. It's Uncle Charles we're talking about. Uncle Charles didn't like Henry's getting killed. Uncle Charles can't take it. Uncle Charles was devoted to Henry, and Henry's death has upset him. That's what Mother says and she ought to know. She's been in his room trying to keep him from killing himself, with poison taken out of the downstairs liquor chest, ever since he started off before I got home from here last night—or this morning. Charles is in one of his cycles. Down grade or up grade, whichever you want to call it."

"But your father——"

He nodded. "My father took the policemen over because he didn't want to say in front of our two neighbors that Uncle Charles was fried to the eyebrows. The Cavanaughs stick to the Cavanaughs and the Beckwiths . . . the Beckwiths stick to the Cavanaughs. By definition. That's why Mother is shipping us off to the Island. She doesn't want you to know. Or me, any more than I have to."

He lighted a cigarette and jammed the lighter viciously shut.

"The Beckwiths are proud people, my girl. The Beckwiths have been too damned good to associate with a lousy climber like Andrea Huse-Lorne for five solid years. They'd prefer not to give her the pleasure of going to her meeting this morning and telling all the bluest bloods in Nassau that poor dear Eleanor's brother was too potted, early in the morning, to show at the inquiry into his own boatman's unfortunate death from the same causes, and it was a frightful mistake for her to let the Beckwiths through the wall in the second place. It's all as plain as the nose on your sweet, pretty face that I'm absolutely nuts about. I love you, Betsy . . . I really do."

"Don't, please . . ." She pushed him gently away from her, laughing as she did it. Then her face sobered instantly.

"I'm sorry."

"Don't be sorry about it. Let's hope the sight of a couple

114

of semi-military gendarmes will snap him out of it. You can't ever tell. He was the one wanted an investigation. Now they're making one he might feel better about it. But . . . let's go back a ways. Why did you want to know if Uncle Charles ever drove a cab?"

She looked at him uncertainly, with a bewildered shake of her head. "I don't know, really. Not now. Except that for a moment I . . . I thought . . ."

She shook her head again, like the mockingbird outside shaking the water from the pool off his feathers.

"I really don't know. It was sort of a hallucination . . . I guess you'd call it. But for a minute I thought . . . Perhaps it's because your Uncle Charles has been in my mind so much. Because I suppose they're nothing alike, really. I . . . just now, since I remembered about Harriet, and that she had a beau, I could see him again. I can see him clearly now. He was very big, and he had a big nose and shoe-polish black hair. It's funny, but I can see him much more clearly, now, than I can her. I thought he was divine. He was a secret I had with Harriet, because when it was her turn to take me to the movies we used to sneak off to Hoboken, where his cab stand was. Oh, I remember now—and I'd forgotten all about it!"

She laughed suddenly, her eyes shining.

"We'd ride around and eat hot dogs. I was sick once, but I never told on her. It was the most exciting thing that ever happened to me."

She still could not get the trailing image of Charles Cavanaugh out of her mind. The two faces, so different, seemed to merge into one the moment she quit consciously thinking how different they were. Scott watched her intently through the casual curl of his cigarette smoke.

"Let me ask you something, Betsy," he said, very gravely. "Why has my Uncle Charles been so much in your mind?"

She started a little, caught a long distance off, thinking about the two men. Her cheeks flushed warmly.

"I don't know. I don't know why I said it."

He took her hand and held it firmly in his. "Listen, Betsy. I think you do. This is no time to hold off anything. I've told you what I think about Charles. Come on, honey—out with it. What is it about him that's upset you so?"

When she sat there silently he took her chin in his hand and held her face up to him.

"Betsy . . . Listen to me. I said this is no time to pull any

115

punches. I couldn't mean it any more. Somebody did try to poison you, last night. The tablet in that bottle of yours is cyanide. I took it over to the Hospital this morning and a guy I know there ran a test on it for me. Maybe you can play Russian roulette once . . . but this wasn't even that. They didn't give you a chance to whirl the barrel. We take this to the police—but I want to talk to Dad first. He's a useful man when there's trouble. And I've got to know about things, first. Don't you see, Betsy? And you're very important to me . . . really important. Much more important than anybody else."

She looked at him for a moment, then went over to the dresser, got the iris-tinted letter out of it, brought it back and gave it to him.

"I don't know what else to do but tell you," she said simply. "I . . . I suppose I'm accusing your uncle. I . . . I don't know anything else to think."

If Charles Cavanaugh was the taxi driver, he and Harriet Grantson could be the They Henry had talked about, and Henry could have been hanging on . . .

She put the rest of it out of her mind. It was for Scott to decide. Her heart shrank to a smaller size as she watched him read Mary Davis's letter, his face more somber the deeper into it he got. After all, Charles was his uncle. Even when he was saying Uncle Charles meant nothing to him, it was obvious he was saying it because Uncle Charles meant a great deal to him and to all of them. And Andrea Huse-Lorne had warned her not to say anything. Families clung together. The instant an outsider attacked, they drew up the ranks closer than before.

She went across the room and stood looking blindly out into the sunlit garden. She saw his mother hurry across the upstairs veranda and go into a room there. Her brother's room. *The Cavanaughs stick to the Cavanaughs, and the Beckwiths . . . the Beckwiths stick to the Cavanaughs. By definition. Like two plus two equals. You know.* A sort of special misery stirred inside her. *I'd rather be dead than lose him now. I really would. But I'm just a Dayton. Nobody has to stick to me.*

But if Scott did not stick to her now, she was gone. If he told his parents, or his Uncle Charles . . .

I wish I'd never told him. I wish I'd just kept still.

But if she could not trust Scott, she had nobody to trust at all.

116

17

Scott Beckwith went rapidly through the gate in the pink wall. The image of Betsy as he'd left her was sharp in his mind—backed against the dressing table, her chin up, her eyes hostile, as both of them had suddenly flared into senseless anger at each other.

"I didn't want to tell you—you insisted! I know it sounds crazy. You needn't keep saying it! You told me to try to think of everything I could, and when I do, you tell me I must be out of my head! Mary Davis isn't out of her head! Your uncle did write to Mr. Steinberg. Henry did write me that note. It's not my fault it all seems tied up with your Uncle Charles. I just don't want to wake up dead some morning, and just because you don't want to believe that an uncle of yours . . ."

He'd left her then, angry himself, angry because he was frightened, and a lot more frightened than she was, it seemed to him. He had taken refuge in anger not only because he was frightened but because of the sudden picture in his mind of Charles down under the bougainvilleas, in the early hours of the morning, blasting and cursing Henry's sniveling soul to eternal damnation. It seemed to have some ghastly incomprehensible kind of catalytic effect on the whole thing, giving it a possibility of truth that was too circumstantially evident to reject and too unbelievably horrible for him to accept without fighting it violently every inch of the way. The stubborn set of her jaw, the hot, defensive gleam in her eyes as she said she knew she was wrong, she must be wrong, about the cab driver, gave it the double lie. Each time she denied it, he knew she was becoming more passionately convinced in her own mind. And he had to find out. Sure, it was crazy . . . but if Charles Cavanaugh hadn't been as near crazy as nothing down there early that morning, then Scott Beckwith was close to the borderline himself.

His father was not on the porch or in the living room and

117

not likely to be upstairs. He went across to the steps and looked down on the lower level. It was where he had talked to Charles. His father was down there, sitting on the bamboo chaise, his cold pipe in his hand, the morning paper on his knees, looking off over the red and gray rooftops toward the bay. If there was any other way, Scott would have chosen it gladly. If there was any other way to answer the crawling, peculiarly sickening questions that made him feel that gooseflesh was crinkling up and down his spine as he started down the steps, he would have taken it. His father already had enough to put up with without this added to it.

As he went down the steps, John Beckwith turned his head. Scott could see him draw in his breath, deeply and with a kind of profound frustration and weariness, as he put his paper aside and started to get up. It was as if he were saying, "All right, what is it now?" Then as he saw Scott's face he stared for an instant and got up more rapidly, alert to something more critically acute than he had presumed from past experience.

"What is it, Scott?"

"It's about Betsy."

Now he was there, he didn't know how to approach it. He seemed to be on some fantastic wheel that was flinging him to opposite poles, flashing extremes of this can't make sense, this does make sense . . . this is too crazy to believe, this really happened and you've got to believe it. He took the soiled, torn sheet of note paper with Henry's illiterate scrawl on it out of his pocket, and the typed iris-tinted letter from the girl at the office.

"I couldn't be sorrier to bother you now, Dad," he said earnestly. "But this is terribly serious. Do you know about the Dayton business? Betsy's father?"

John Beckwith nodded. "I'd forgotten it until they were talking about it next door, last evening, when Betsy was in the house. I remembered there was a good deal of whispering. I didn't listen to it. As far as we'd looked into it, there was no question about Dayton's personal reputation. Why?"

"Because . . ." He stopped. "I'd better tell you first that I'm going to marry Betsy. You'll see in a minute why I think I ought to tell you right off."

His father put his hand on his shoulder. "Good. That's very good, Scott—I'm glad to hear it. But that's not what's disturbing you, is it."

118

"No. It's the Dayton business. There's . . . there's something pretty bad going on around here. Let me tell you this first. The New York police thought the fire that burned the money and killed the secretary in the warehouse was accidental, but that Dayton was getting ready to skip out with the cash, taking his secretary along, and didn't die of a heart attack but killed himself when he saw the game was up. That's the way they taped it. But read this."

He gave his father the soiled torn piece of hotel stationery with the warning scrawled on it, and watched the startled and incredulous expression that came into John Beckwith's face as he read it, and read it a second and a third time.

John Beckwith looked at Scott silently.

"There was a tablet of cyanide in her aspirin bottle," Scott said. "It was put there after she got here. She got the bottle at the airport. I had the tablet tested at the Hospital this morning. This is unbelievable, of course, Dad, but it happens to be true."

It seemed to him that his father's face was quite expressionless as he nodded slightly. He saw then the somber anxiety, dread even, that seemed to be dawning slowly on him, as if it were a peculiar contagion spreading to him from his son. Scott kept his eyes fixed steadily on the iris-tinted letter in his hands as he went on.

"Henry put that warning under her door, last night. Before he drowned—or was drowned—in the cistern. There's a question here that we've got to answer. Why should Henry be warning Betsy? How could he have had any connection with the Dayton affair? Who else is here—if anybody—who was connected with it?"

John Beckwith looked steadily at him, waiting.

"Or who'd connect Betsy with it in the first place, or be interested in her being here?"

He was still not looking at his father, but he felt him move slightly, as if closing into some special field of his own. Looking around at him then, he saw the troubled lines deepen around his eyes and at the corners of his mouth.

"What I mean is," he said quietly, "how can we explain this?"

He handed his father the typed letter with the irises flaunting themselves across it, and watched him, aware, with some surprise, that the element of shock he had expected John Beckwith to show, reading it, was somehow missing.

"Did you . . . you didn't know this?"

119

John Beckwith shook his head. "I knew Charles got a letter from Betsy's office yesterday. It was the one you got at the Post Office. He . . . burned it, and buried the ashes in the cape jasmine tub up there."

They were both silent for a moment. It was a full and intense silence, vibrating as sharply as sound between them. John Beckwith looked at his son questioningly. "Go on," he said. "I take it there's more."

"One of the employees," Scott said quietly, "a bookkeeper and assistant to the secretary who was burned to death in the fire, disappeared right afterwards. Nobody has ever heard of her since. Her office was next to the chemists' laboratory and stockroom. She was the one who got Dayton's prescription for his heart tablets filled that morning and delivered it to him. Betsy says that was added to the police files. She never thought what it could mean until . . . this."

He touched Henry's note lying there between them.

"Her name was Harriet Grantson."

"Grantson."

Scott nodded. "That's right. And Harriet had a beau. Betsy remembered him, after she'd tried to think back to all this, when she got that note that Henry left there, and after she'd found that tablet in her aspirin bottle that wasn't marked like all the others. And she remembers Harriet Grantson's beau clearly, now—better than she does Harriet Grantson. In fact, she's dead sure of him."

He paused an instant and added, "He drove a taxicab." He looked up then, directly to his father, hesitating again, even at this point so close to what he had to ask. "Dad . . . I know this sounds about as cockeyed as you can get, but here it is. Did Uncle Charles ever drive a cab . . . in Hoboken, in 1939? I know it . . ."

He stopped, his breath catching sharply, staring at his father's face. It was as gray as the stone paving the terrace under his feet. His lips were gray. John Beckwith looked tired, suddenly, terribly tired, his hands trembling like an old man's as he fumbled with the tobacco pouch filling his pipe. He did not have to speak.

"Did he have a love affair with a girl named Harriet?" Scott asked steadily.

His father sat without speaking for a moment. When he answered, he managed a semblance of his normal self.

"Let me answer your last question first, Scott." He even managed the semblance of a smile. "I should be exceedingly surprised if he had not. I don't mean I knew about this particular love affair . . . but with Harriet, or Jane, or Molly Ann. Their names have never been important. Or not till now." He looked at Scott questioningly. "And don't misunderstand me. I don't see, quite, what you're leading up to. Charles did drive a cab there—under unusual circumstances. There was nothing discreditable about it. Quite the contrary. It was one of Charles's best periods."

He was silent for a moment, thinking about it.

"I found it out quite by accident. I was in town late one night. We hadn't been seeing anything of him, so I went to his apartment to see him, and ask if he could put me up. The night watchman let me in. After a few minutes a Navy captain came in, and a little later Charles. But . . . I'd never have recognized him if I'd seen him on the street. He was working for Naval Intelligence in the dives and along the waterfront. It was where most of the information about convoys and ship sailings was leaking out to enemy submarines. If you remember, we weren't in the war then, but we weren't out of it. Charles was over there all winter and spring, and I gathered he did a first-rate job. It needed somebody who was quick with his fists as well as his head. Charles has never spoken about it and neither have I. But that is what he was doing there. If he was carrying on a . . . a love affair, it doesn't surprise me at all. It probably helped make his rôle convincing as well as amuse him."

John Beckwith looked steadily at his son. "But that Charles Cavanaugh had any part in the murder of Jerome Dayton, if that's what you're really asking, I could never bring myself to believe. Nor what would seem to be a necessary assumption here, that Henry Grantson was hanging on to him as a blackmailer. That, I could believe even less. Charles could have crushed him out like a paper match box and tossed him into Long Island Sound a hundred times with nobody the wiser."

He got slowly to his feet.

"I've thought a great many things about your uncle, Scott . . . but I have never thought he was either a liar or a cheat. I wouldn't put murder beyond him, if the necessity arose for him to murder anyone—but he would never use poison."

He took up the newspaper and folded it precisely. "However, this situation, no matter how . . . unpleasant, can't be allowed to go further. I don't believe your Uncle Charles is too far gone at this point not to be able to understand what

121

is being said to him. If he is ever that far gone, in fact. I've often doubted it. I am going up there now. If you want to come with me, we'll ask him. If he can't answer the questions you have asked me . . ."

John Beckwith stopped for an instant, and went steadily on.

"—We'll go to the police. Betsy is more important, now, than anything else I know about."

He gave Scott a bleak smile.

"I'd be glad if you'd come. I can't pretend I'm physically able to cope with Charles, if he happens to be in one of his belligerent moods."

"Right," Scott said. He drew a deep breath, knowing his father was not joking. Charles would be gentle as a baby lamb or savage as a maddened bull. He had no middle ground. The cagey cunning was true whether he was violent or peaceful. He thought about that uneasily. Everything his father had said of Charles was true. But there was still that part of him . . . and when the Dayton affair, was rigged, a desperate cunning must have been at work. He thought of the two suitcases, Dayton's and the crabbed secretary's, together at the airport. A cunning of a special order, together with a kind of feline humor . . . of the sort that might have made Charles Cavanaugh's romance with Miss Harriet Grantson a cat-and-rat business that was probably right up Charles's alley? It made him a little nauseated even to think about it.

18

Ramsey Huse-Lorne moved in a room of horror that was his own mind. It was a room of many doors, each one, as he opened it, letting in some new and terrible ray of awful light that no matter how quickly he slammed the door shut was still inside, not to be put out, and not to be denied, no matter how blindly he tried not to look at it and not to believe its presence there. The false lips and false smile. The tiny strands of black silk thread clinging to the carved interstices of the blue lapis ball. The rubber-soled shoes put in the farthest corner of her dressing room closet. The midnight blue robe with the wadded, navy-blue scarf in the pocket, its hem in front spotted with water and dark, iron-brown specks he dared not think more about.

He stood by the stand at the side of her bed. Her leather engagement book was by the telephone on the lower shelf. He opened it to that day and looked at it. Luncheon and bridge at the Balmoral Club at one o'clock. Nothing at all in the space beside ten o'clock. On the next page, the page for tomorrow, in the ten o'clock space, was written "Gymkhana Committee, Government House." That was the meeting she'd said she was going to now, that she'd left the house pretending she was going to. It was not the kind of mistake Andrea would make. She never made mistakes of any kind, in fact. He'd often thought what an excellent secretary she'd have made, with her precise, indelible memory, her machine-like efficiency. But why should she have said that? She must have some reason for wanting to get out of the house. But why? Where could she have to go that made it important for nobody to ask where, and nobody to offer to go along with her, as he might have done if she'd said the market, or Bay Street, or the post office?

He put the book back and went out onto the veranda. He had the quartz lapis ball in his hand, and he stood there, looking about, bewildered. The instinct to hide it was so strong that he looked furtively around him before he went down the stairs. He went across the garden. The compost heap. It was his own special project that no one else was allowed to touch. He slipped into the slat house and got a garden fork. Outside, as the light shone on it, he frowned irritably. Someone had used it and had not cleaned it. He held it up to wipe off the muck and frowned again. Grass clippings had dried on it. He looked at his compost pile and went over to it, looking sharply around, then, at the servants' quarters. Someone had been tampering with it too, and Ramsay Huse-Lorne, whose compost pile represented a symbolic custodianship, the effort to conserve and return something to the rocky substratum drained by centuries of misuse, felt a bumbling flush of indignation. It increased when he saw the spot that had been tampered with. Yesterday's sweepings of dried grass and palm leaves that he had put there carefully had been raised and then flattened down, so that no air could get between them. He stuck the fork in and lifted a layer of it. He had not intended turning the pile again until the summer rains came. The lapis lazuli ball would be safe there.

He lifted the forkful and stopped. A black thing was hanging to it. He shook the leaves and grass off, turning the thing up on the tines of the fork to look at it. It was a stocking, a black silk stocking. He took it off and put the fork down. It was laddered and torn. He stood there, not moving, for several moments, conscious of nothing, actually, except the leaden weight of the lapis ball in his jacket pocket. It was heavier than lead. It was heavier than any ball of lead could ever be. The picture that had been in his mind when he had picked it up first was there again. It was not the picture of himself with the ball wrapped in a napkin, showing his friends the simple trick of how to crush in an enemy's skull with a twist of the wrist . . . it was Andrea, afterwards, after their guests were gone, wrapping it in the trailing chiffon scarf of her dinner dress, saying, "Wonderful, darling. Come the native uprising, I shan't have to bother with a gun. I can use a gun, but I loathe the things. This is divine . . . it wouldn't make a *sound*, would it?"

He held the black stocking in his hand, sicker at heart than he had ever in his life been, and started violently as he heard someone in the garden behind him. He leaned forward quickly to put the stocking back, and for one awful moment thought he was going to pitch forward and fall there himself.

124

He had seen the other one. The mate to the black stocking he held in his hand. It was torn and laddered too. He stared half-blindly for an instant from one to the other. Two. There were two of them. He thrust the one he held into the hole, not waiting to grasp the fork, and with his hands raked the sodden leaves over it and pulled the dry covering up from the side of the heap. He tamped it down with a sharp movement of his foot, and turned then, wiping the streaming sweat from his forehead with the back of his hand.

It was the Dayton girl, there by the pool, watching him, smiling at him.

"Are you a compost addict too?" she asked, laughing. "I have a cousin who's one. He puts old bones and everything but tin cans in."

"Oh, really?" Ramsay Huse-Lorne said.

He spoke so stiffly that she thought she had offended him. Why compost heapers were all such a humorless lot she did not know. They probably just did not think compost heaps were funny. She watched him meticulously cleaning off the tines of his fork before he took it over to the slat house by the sapodilla tree. She hesitated and moved back a little. Perhaps he regarded her as intrusive. Being in his cottage didn't give her any right to come over into the rest of the place, and the English were odd about some things. She went back a little farther as he came back out of the slat house.

"I say, don't go," he said awkwardly. "Sit a bit, won't you?"

She stopped, looking at him. His face was red and perspiring, but there was something in it that looked almost pleading, as if he'd really like her to stay.

"I'm afraid you're rather busy."

"Not at all. As a matter of fact, I'm frightfully sort of . . . at loose ends, you know. Usually I play golf, at this time in the morning. But I'm rather . . . off my feed, I expect. Do sit down. I'll see if there's a spot of coffee."

He came back bringing a small tray with coffee and a jug of hot milk, and put it down for her to pour.

"This is the only time of day I really enjoy the stuff," he said. He lapsed into silence then, and sat there until he stirred abruptly. "I say, you know—this isn't being a particularly happy holiday for you, is it?"

He seemed to be almost apologizing to her, as if in some way it was his fault and he was sorry for it.

"It's nice just not having to get up and be at my desk at

nine every morning." She smiled at him. There was something very appealing and even moving about his sad eyes and long, drooping face, and something that shone out of it, that she had felt even when she talked to him the first time, something enormously kind and really good there, in an ungainly and inarticulate way. And something in herself responded to it, making her suddenly, to her surprise at first, want to talk to him, and tell him everything, as if he'd understand, as Scott hadn't understood. The minor wound in her heart at the way Scott had made her go over everything a hundred times, as if he thought she was just a hysterical child, imagining half of it, was still unhealed. And the way he'd walked off and left her, both of them angry, but with her not knowing whether he was only angry, or frightened too, frightened and worried out of his mind, as she was. And he'd been gone so long . . . It was because she couldn't bear staying any longer by herself there that she'd come out, and seeing Major Huse-Lorne had come over, so she wouldn't have to be by herself, going endlessly over the same ground, like a rat in a globular maze, too blind or too stupid to find a way out of it.

Not that she wanted to break down and tell Ramsay Huse-Lorne all her troubles. But one thing she did want to tell him. The desire had come to her that morning, when they were on the veranda outside the blue-and-gold drawing room, when Colonel Renfrew was there. Somehow, it didn't matter about Mrs. Huse-Lorne, but it did matter about him, because he was . . . the only word she could think of was just decent.

"Would you mind if I told you something, Major Huse-Lorne?"

She heard herself saying it before she knew she'd made up her mind, really, to say it. He waited, as if he felt the curious warmth of sympathy in her that she felt in him.

"It's about my father. Your wife told me yesterday that Mr. Cavanaugh had told you all about him, when he was over here. But it . . . it's not true. I know it, now. He . . . he didn't kill himself."

She looked at him earnestly. He seemed startled, unusually startled, but he would, of course.

"He didn't plan to steal his friends' money and run off with his secretary. They were both . . . they were both killed."

"Oh, I say!" He put down his coffee cup, blinking at her.

"I know it sounds funny, for me to talk about it . . . but it's . . . oh, you don't know how great a relief, knowing he wasn't a thief, and a coward."

He seemed to be trying to say something, but she didn't notice.

"I still haven't any idea who did it," she said. "It seems so unbelievable. But there was another person in my father's office that nobody has ever heard of again. I don't suppose Mr. Cavanaugh told you about her. That's the queer thing about all of it. Her name was Harriet Grantson, and that man who drowned last night—you remember his name was Grantson too. He was the one who told me about my father. He put a note under my door last night. That's how I found it out."

She looked over at him then. "I suppose it seems silly, but I thought I'd like you to know my father didn't do what everybody's always thought he did. I don't think Mr. Cavanaugh was trying to hurt me, telling you people, but . . ."

It was clear she was making Major Huse-Lorne extremely uncomfortable. He was moving unhappily in his chair, as if he wanted to deny Mr. Cavanaugh had even talked about her but couldn't get his tongue to work to do it.

"I say," he stammered at last, "my wife didn't . . . I mean to say, she *really* didn't tell you that——"

"She wasn't telling me to make me feel badly about anything," Betsy said quickly. "I mean, about my father, or even about Mr. Cavanaugh." Her eyes widened a little as she looked at him. He obviously hadn't understood it the way she meant it. "And she didn't actually tell me."

He seemed so relieved that perhaps she shouldn't have gone on.

"It was just because she was so upset herself at that nice man who started talking about my father, that she told me about it at all," she said. "I'd thought she was annoyed at me, the way she looked, and that's what she wanted to explain. She said she was sure Mr. Cavanaugh had told you about it so I'd escape being embarrassed and unhappy. And of course she was right, about Scott's uncle—it's natural he should be antagonistic toward me."

Her own antagonism toward Charles Cavanaugh flared suddenly, bright and burning. "Although I don't think that's any excuse for him to——"

She flashed her hand up to her mouth, appalled and shocked at herself, on the very verge of saying "—to open

127

my mail." Her eyes met Major Huse-Lorne's staring at her. He was shocked enough already, shocked into even more inarticulate speechlessness apparently than he'd had before.

It was not Betsy Dayton that Huse-Lorne was shocked at. He was appalled, and had been from the moment she'd started to talk about Cavanaugh, at the disparity, hideous under the circumstances, between what Andrea had conveyed to her of what Cavanaugh had said and the account he'd actually given. It was not so much that there had been no antagonism in Cavanaugh's account, quite the contrary, rather. Though why had Andrea allowed the girl to think he'd been unfriendly? And why had she gone into such a frozen fury at the man talking about her father? He had seen that himself. No, it was more, much more, than that. How did his wife, who knew no Daytons except casual yachtsmen, and who knew nothing at all about Betsy, know so much more about what her father was supposed to have done than Cavanaugh had told her?

Plain fear crawled in his heart as he tried to think it out. His mind stopped at still another point, and then another, and another. In an extraordinary way, so many things that had been inexplicable about her suddenly began to weave themselves together into a clearly patterned whole . . . and a kind of horrible illumination it was beginning to cast, Huse-Lorne thought with almost unbearable dread . . . like a thundering red dawn breaking angrily on the horizon of his mind. Small and unimportant things about her past life, in contrast to the open book that was his own. Grantson. He spoke the word silently. The initial "G." It was strange the incident had stayed in his mind, except that it was the first indication of the blazing temper she'd so remarkably concealed when he was first married to her. It was a filmy white nightdress with a big lacy "G" embroidered on it. He'd picked it up, pleased with the soft femininity of it, and she'd flown at him, practically tearing it out of his hands, and then explained, contritely and tearfully, that it had belonged to a dead friend. He suppressed the groan that almost came to his lips, thinking about Charles Cavanaugh's visit, that had seemed so annoying, at the time, but so entirely normal, and the bewildering sense he'd had, later on, of some kind of what the Americans called doubletalk going on. And seeing Andrea's drawn, green smile.

He groaned inwardly again. Cavanaugh, at the bar last night. Adroitly questioning him, and him letting go and

128

telling all about his meeting Andrea, his marriage to her, her holdings, all of it. He raised his eyes and let them rest on the tree-screened open veranda of the Beckwith house across the pink-plastered wall. Andrea must think, now, that Cavanaugh was not interested in her . . . but she must have thought he was interested when he called. He could see her in his mind, sitting frozen in her chair as the fellow got up to leave.

What had happened, what was happening now? She must have changed her mind some time later. He remembered the kind of exulting triumph that he'd presumed was because she'd got the Beckwiths to her cocktail party, and that was what had driven him out of the house to collapse like a bleating, maundering fool in the vine leaves and barley Cavanaugh had heaped on him while he pumped him like a well. Grantson . . . Andrea, his wife . . . creeping down into the dark places of the garden to talk to him, and slipping back. Lying to him, to Renfrew. "G" for Grantson. Harriet Grantson had disappeared, never been heard of since. It was all tenuous, all involved; but because he had been so in love with her, so passionately interested, once, in every thread of her life, and because there were so few threads, he had gathered them tenderly. And the cloth they wove now, even the invisible ones he'd forgotten, consciously forgotten, but that were there again now, part of the fabric lying in his hands, was a dark and horrible thing. And somehow, he'd known there was something in her past that she kept hidden. Small contradictions, memories that would suddenly light in her eyes that would go blank before she'd say, "Nothing, darling." She had never once gone back to the States, never to New York, even to Miami. And the nightmares she had had when they were first married and her room still opened into his. He shuddered a little, remembering some of them.

Above all, the second stocking, over there in the compost heap.

The agony churned in the pit of his stomach. But Betsy Dayton was looking at him, and he jolted himself. It seemed a long time he had been sunk there, reliving his life with Andrea, the threads weaving in the loom of his mind, making the last loops and turns that showed the pattern, as the last few bright stitches bring out the figures in a square of gros point. It had not been long in time . . . as the mind can flash instantly from London to Bangkok to Singapore as the body would take weeks or years of living to move there.

"I'm dreadfully sorry!" she was saying. "I don't know what possessed me to tell you——"

As he looked across the little table at her, another figure in the woven pattern flashed sharply out, and he saw at once, with an indescribable sinking of his heart, that it was the central figure. The girl. Jerome Dayton's daughter. He recalled seeing her as she was first coming to the cottage, and calling back to Andrea. She'd gone at once to her room and left the guest list on the desk in the drawing room, with "Girl" written on it. She hadn't known her name. That was when, going up there, he'd seen her horribly green and raddled face through the slats of the blinds. And he'd offered to send for a doctor . . .

He looked at Betsy with appalled desperation. This was the occasion of the second stocking.

"Forgive me, please!" She'd put down her coffee cup and got to her feet. "I must go. I've kept you from your gardening. Don't get up."

He was having a hard time getting his long bony arms and legs collected, trying to pull himself out of the chair.

"I say," he said. "Really, you mustn't feel——"

But she was gone, her face flushed. As she ran up the cottage steps she looked back and saw him sitting there still, staring in front of him.

19

"Oh, dear heavens!" she thought wretchedly . . . *Just let anybody look kindly at her and she pours her heart out.* It was a wonder she'd stopped where she did, hadn't told him all the rest, about Charles opening her mail, and what she'd said to Scott, practically accusing his uncle of trying to murder her, of having actually murdered her father and old Miss Gurney as well as carrying on a love affair with Harriet Grantson. She crept to the window and looked back across the garden. Major Huse-Lorne started to get up and sank back, staring across the garden towards his compost heap. He'd had something he'd planned to do, and she'd sat there being so . . . so incredible that he'd lost the heart to go on working. No wonder the English thought Americans had no manners.

But she felt better. Just getting some of it out of her system made her feel much better than she had when she went over there. She could even go to the mirror and look at herself and put on some lipstick. Then she went to the door. Scott and his father were going up the steps to the upstairs veranda. Her heart stood still an instant. She turned back into the cottage. They were going up to talk to Charles Cavanaugh, of course. To tell him . . . She stood there, intensely unhappy . . . and yet her conviction, instead of fading out of her mind, becoming more solid and more determined there.

Charles Cavanaugh *was* the taxi driver. She went across the room to get her hat and bag, and stopped half-way across as a flash of illumination came sharply to her. Charles Cavanaugh was the taxi driver. She knew now. What she remembered, what had actually made her think of it first, was the unmistakable hunch of those extraordinary shoulders over the table at the Carlton Bar when he was talking to Henry, and again, the same tough, heavy line of them down on the terrace there, his head lowered as he knelt over Henry

Grantson's body. The picture of them, years ago, was intensely vivid now in her mind. Harriet Grantson was not. She could not bring her face into her mind at all, in fact, except as a shadowy thing with dark hair and a scarf tied around it, her hat on the back seat with Betsy while they rode around, and Harriet wanting him to kiss her but he wouldn't. *Not while the kid's here.* The very words flashed into her mind too.

But . . . it was a queer thing. It was the excitement of it, her first impact with sex, the psychiatrists would probably say, that made the memory so much clearer than hundreds of nicer, more properly to be remembered experiences of her childhood. They'd probably say she was in love with him herself. Maybe they'd be right. She laughed a little. They'd probably say that was why she fell in love with Scott so instantly—because he was in so many ways so like his uncle. The past kept on flooding into her mind. While Miss Gurney was sick she'd been with Harriet a lot of times. She remembered, with a slight shock, wishing on the first star at night that poor Miss Gurney would be in the hospital a long time so she and Harriet could keep on being together. Keeping it a secret from her father and Miss Gurney was part of the reason it was so exciting . . . Miss Gurney trying to pump her, Harriet making up stories for them to tell, on the way back. And the wonderful joke of paying the taxi driver with Miss Gurney pretending not to watch from the window. She could see him now, from the back seat, grumpily looking at the change they handed him for a tip, winking at her under the pulled-down visor of his old cap before he stuck the change in his pocket and leaned forward a little—with those shoulders—to give the flag a bang up again before he drove off down the crowded street.

It was not a coordinated sequence of any kind but isolated moments that she could bring back and see, with Harriet always so shadowy a figure in them that she must really have thought it was herself, not Harriet, who was the true heroine of the piece.

Her face sobered as she remembered why she was recalling it. She picked up her hat and bag. There was no use staying here waiting; she could at least go down to Bay Street. Actually she knew that what she was doing was running away, getting out of the cottage before Scott and his father came out of Charles Cavanaugh's room. She didn't dare think what was happening before. And even if he was her taxi

132

driver—— She stopped short. That was the queer thing. She'd almost forgotten it. He'd been much too nice to her for him to . . . She'd thought he was wonderful. He couldn't possibly . . . But that made less sense than any of the rest. How could a ten-year-old girl know?

She put on her sun hat and started to the door. Then she went back to the dressing table and got a pair of white gloves. Mrs. Huse-Lorne had had gloves. Perhaps colonial standards in Bay Street were higher than they were in other resorts. She started out again, came back a second time, took off one glove and scribbled a note. "Gone down to Bay Street to shop and get out of everybody's hair." She smiled and added, "Back soon. Love, B." She left it just inside the door. She didn't want him to worry about her if he came back and found her gone.

Ramsay Huse-Lorne looked back from the door of the slat house, looking up once more at the shelf holding his potted orchids, dormant for the winter. He had put the quartz lapis lazuli ball back of them. As he came on out, he saw Betsy Dayton. Hat, bag, and gloves. In Nassau that meant Bay Street. And in Bay Street . . . He brushed the moss off his hands and hurried across the garden, up the stairs and along the veranda to his room.

She must not meet Andrea in Bay Street . . . A silent prayer was on his lips as he tore off his soiled, sweat-stained shirt and shorts and put on fresh ones, clumsy desperation goading his awkward hands. He breathed rapidly as he hastily brushed his lank blond hair and hurried through the hall and out. She was just at the bottom of the road turning down toward the Square. He quickened his long, bouncing stride. She must not meet Andrea. The second stocking was like an evil omen hanging on the latchstring of his mind. Andrea would be in her car, he thought suddenly. He brushed rudely past a friend who stopped to talk to him and hurried on down the hill. Everyone in Nassau met everyone else in Bay Street. Betsy Dayton must not meet Andrea there. As he turned the corner he saw both of them, Andrea coming from Rawson Square, Betsy stopped in front of a small group of straw-work women, their hats and baskets piled against a wall. He saw the blue car parked at the curb, and Andrea quickening her steps.

The flow of traffic between him and them was a sudden maddening welter of motor cars, horns tooting, carriage bells

133

ringing. He was across the road from them, half a long, crowded block away. He barged out into the road, and lost sight of them as a horse-drawn carriage tinkled gaily between him and them. When he saw them again, they were together, moving back toward the car. Faces—black, white, and brown—blurred before his eyes, voices glanced in meaningless jumble off his ears. He heard his name, flapped his hands and rushed disjointedly on. He'd look a perfect ass if he ran, and yet if he did not run he'd never make it. Andrea would not stop, of course, when he called to her. She was already getting in behind the wheel, Betsy Dayton was bending over to get in beside her. He wasn't going to make it. He knew it. And he couldn't shout . . . to save Betsy . . . and, more poignantly to himself even then, to save Andrea. The truth about her was finally his . . . an evil thing, stalking, darkly terrible, beside him in the soft laughter and gaiety of the sunlit street.

Charles Cavanaugh was sitting in the chintz-covered chair, his back to the slanting half-shut louvres, his hands resting on the upholstered arms, his clean-shaven chin down on his chest. He was in his pajamas and cotton dressing gown, his feet in the rope-soled beach shoes. His blue eyes, half open, were glazed, but the rest of his youthful, unlined face was happily settled into a childlike smile. He was quiet and peaceful, escaped from the rigorous world into his pleasant valley, not yet arrived at the dark precipice at the end of its treacherous and insubstantial declining slopes. Scott closed the door, not looking at him at once. It was always painful, seeing him lost in his vapidly smiling oblivion. It was more painful now. He was still thinking about what his father had said as they started up the porch steps, when he had stopped and turned a troubled face to him.

"Do you realize something? . . . that your Uncle Charles did not become a pathological drinker until sometime that year? I was thinking about it this morning, trying to remember when he quit drinking in a civilized fashion and started on this sort of thing." John Beckwith was thinking beyond that, as he spoke, to Charles during the war, and what had seemed his almost determined will to die. "I was wondering. Could it be some kind of a profound sense of guilt . . . ?"

"That might be why we've never been able to get him to a psychiatrist."

Scott wondered too. That was a vivid recurrent part of
134

their life with Charles Cavanaugh. Trying to get him to go to a clinic to straighten himself out. His almost childish terror, his promises if they wouldn't make him go . . . a sickening sort of business, always ending and always beginning. But if that was the basic cause . . . He looked at him now, thankful as he saw his imperturbable, placid smile that he was in this mood, not the other. Nevertheless he went on to where he could be between Charles and his father if one of the lightning changes from lamb to gored, raving bull took place, or he saw the mild, happy smile turn slowly into the mean, cunning watchfulness that sometimes came before the transformation. He looked at his father, sitting calmly on Charles's freshly-made bed, filling his pipe. He hoped he knew what he was doing. He had had experience enough.

"Charles," John Beckwith said thoughtfully, "I wonder if you'd help us out with a problem we've got."

Charles Cavanaugh nodded. "Glad to help," he mumbled. "Always glad to help an old friend. Sorry can't offer you a drink, old friend. Sister doesn't allow. Fine woman, my sister. Prejudiced. But fine woman. Don't say anything about my sister, old friend."

"She's a very fine woman, Charles," John Beckwith said. "It's another woman we want to ask about."

"Women. Always women." Cavanaugh moved his head slowly. The smile faded off his face. "Stupid, mercenary. No use for 'em. Stupid, mercenary fools. All they are."

"What about Harriet Grantson, Charles?"

Scott felt his heart beat more quickly as he waited for the name to cross the broad, dim prairie and reach into Charles's inner clouded ears, and for the recognition when it finally reached them. It seemed a dangerous way to go at it, if recognition came, but perhaps his father knew more about it than he did. He moved a little nearer, keeping his weight forward.

"Harriet. Harriet Grantson." Charles Cavanaugh repeated the name slowly. "Harriet Grantson."

Scott's heart chilled. He did know her. He had been there, he'd known Harriet Grantson. Betsy was right. But it was in a way merely confirmation. He knew both he and his father had accepted it as the truth. He stood there, his body tensed, not because of what he now knew but watching Charles Cavanaugh's face, bland, unlined, for what would follow, the first sign of danger or of despair.

He repeated the name again, raising his face, looking somewhere far off, and repeated it once more. Then suddenly something happened, and it was there. Not what Scott had expected. Neither violence nor anger, cunning nor meanness. None of those things possessed his face, or contorted it. Instead, it slowly crumpled in front of them. It was like the thin, rubber face of an air-inflated figure, the air that held it seeping out, letting it crumple down into a distorted, lopsided thing half its size. Scott stared, not believing what his eyes saw, and tensed again quickly as Charles Cavanaugh's face swelled back then into shape, but a different shape, darkly suffused, his blond brows drawing together, his thick shoulders hunching forward, his hands coming slowly up, fingers tightening. For an instant Scott thought he was about to spring at John Beckwith's throat. He took another step forward. His father sat there motionless. Cavanaugh brought his clutching fingers together. It was a throat he was clutching, but not John Beckwith's.

"I'll kill her myself."

The blood suffused his face a darker red, the veins standing out on his temples, the cords of his neck swelling into knotted lines. Then, as suddenly, his great body relaxed into flaccid dough, his face crumpled as it had before. Tears gathered in his eyes and rolled down his face onto the cotton dressing gown, spreading out on it in wet splotches. Scott's blood froze as he spoke again.

"I wanted to kill her last night. But not Henry." He raised his voice to a sniveling Cockney whine. " 'Give 'er a chanct, Mr. Cavanaugh. M'ybe it ain't 'er. M'ybe I myde a mistyke. M'ybe it ain't 'er after all, Mr. Cavanaugh.' "

His whole body shook, his hands, working convulsively on the glazed chintz arms of the chair, rasped as his nails dug into the cloth.

"I trusted the white-livered rotten little rat," he sobbed. "I told him how to get in there. I showed him where to go. And what happens? He wouldn't let me kill her. She kills him. I know!"

Scott Beckwith had forgotten this was a potential wild beast. He had forgotten everything, for the instant, in the whirling daze of horror that paralyzed his mind. It couldn't be, but it was. Charles was saying he was going to kill her, she'd killed . . . He felt his heart pounding, the blood rushing to his head.

His father's voice was a sharp whisper. "Scott—sit down!" John Beckwith had not moved. Cavanaugh was still staring blindly in front of him, his nails tearing at the hard chintz on the chair arm.

"Why did you want to kill her, Charles?"

Scott heard the tinge of fear in his father's steady voice, saw the gray line of his lips.

"You don't know." Dry sobs tore Cavanaugh's heavy frame again. "You didn't know. But . . . I took her there. I took her there in my own cab. I knew she was there, waiting inside. I knew Jerome's plans. I drove around the block to wait. I was to come back and pick her up. Then I saw a man I'd been tailing and lost. When I got back the fire engines were there and Dayton was dead. And I knew it was her. All the time I knew . . . and never said anything. I let her get away with it. I let her kill both of them."

He was shaking horribly, trying to back away from it, pushing his chair against the slanted louvres, his face gray and raddled, the vision in his eyes horrible to see, even when no one but himself could see it, fighting it off with his hands, trying to keep it from closing in on him.

"I was glad to get her off my neck," the thick voice mumbled. "I was sick of her mewling and mauling. I didn't care what happened to her . . . hauling the kid along." He sat there shaking. "I let her get away with it. The kid's father. First I didn't know, then I did. Then I let 'em go on thinking he killed himself. I knew. I let her get away with two hundred thousand . . ."

Scott saw his father's hand move quietly, keeping him silent where he was, not to break into the confession unconsciously draining out before them.

"And Henry, Charles?"

"Henry." Cavanaugh's body came forward, his hands hanging limp on his knees again. "Henry." He repeated the name as if it were somebody he had forgotten in the agony of his contrition and remorse. "Henry couldn't find her. He couldn't figure where she'd got to. He went every place, hunting for her. I found him. We figured it out then. He hated her. I gave him the dough to try to find her. He knew the old man had been talking about Nassau. Travel stuff in the office. He figured she might get down here and he found her for me. That's why I bought this place, next door to her, so we could catch her, so she couldn't kill anybody else . . . Then Henry got scared. 'Leave 'er be. She ain't 'urtin' nobody but 'erself. 'Use-Lorne'll see she ain't up to no tricks.' "

How long Scott Beckwith had known it was Andrea Huse-Lorne Charles was talking about, when the She's and Her's sorted themselves out, not to mean Betsy Dayton but to mean Harriet Grantson, to mean Andrea Huse-Lorne . . . when the dawning realization hit him with the impact of all its meaning, he was too dazed and too horror-stricken to know. The mumbling jumble of Charles Cavanaugh's blurred speech as he lapsed into incoherences, the She's and the Her seeming to point first to one person, then to another, first to Betsy, then to Harriet Grantson, had dulled the edge of his own perceptions, and the final, traumatic effect of slapping it all together, in Nassau, slapping it all right there, was like one of Charles Cavanaugh's powerful hands slapping him across the eyes, paralyzing him, blinding him for one long incredible moment.

His father's voice, the thrust of his eyes as he turned them to him, brought him out of the paralysis, the whirl and conflict of the things pouring from Charles Cavanaugh's lips, the bewilderment as he only half followed what his uncle was saying.

"Get Betsy, Scott . . ."

He tore himself out of the half-dazed trance and leaped to the door.

"I thought the girl would know her. I thought——"

He heard that as he jerked the door open . . . the dull voice, Charles burying himself again behind the blank wall of silence. It was hopelessness again in the voice he heard then. "I thought the girl would——"

He raced down the stairs and across the grass to the iron gate in the wall. What Charles had said still whirled, conflicting, incomprehensible, in his mind, as Harriet Grantson seemed to . . . He thrust that out of his mind. Only one thing mattered.

He called Betsy's name, wrenched the door of the cottage open and saw the note on the floor. Bay Street. She'd be safe there. Andrea was at her meeting. Or was she? The sick agony in his heart seemed alternately to freeze it dead and fan it to searing flames. He ran back to the house and through it to the street. If she was in Bay Street he could find her. If she was not . . .

20

Betsy bent forward to get into the car. It would be fun to drive out and see the Country Club. Andrea said it wouldn't take very long—nothing on the tiny island in the middle of the sea could possibly take very long—and it would have the double advantage of keeping her from under the Beckwiths' harried feet and from the temptation of buying a lot of things she couldn't afford and didn't need. There was a wonderful basket there in the pile the native woman had. She stopped, looking around at it again.

"We ought to be getting along if we're going, darling."

It seemed to Betsy there was a touch of impatience in Andrea's voice. She started to get in the car, and saw Ramsay Huse-Lorne coming, almost bolting along Bay Street. There was no mistaking him for anybody else—his straw-blond head and drooping blond mustache, the white shirt and white starched shorts, the hairy sun-reddened knees.

"There comes your husband." She straightened up, waiting for him. "He's terribly sweet, isn't he?" she added impulsively.

Mrs. Huse-Lorne had switched on the engine. She pressed her foot on the gas. "Let's not wait for him, Betsy. He's on his way to the post office. He's terribly sweet but he hates to be interrupted when he's doing anything or going anywhere."

It seemed to Betsy, glancing back again at him, that Huse-Lorne was making for them, rushing along, actually, insofar as he could for the traffic, and looking very much as if he wanted to get to Andrea before she drove off. She couldn't see that, of course, sitting behind the wheel with a car in front of her. Then Betsy knew it was so, because Major Huse-Lorne, seeing she was looking at him, flapped up one big red hand, obviously waving it at her to stop. She leaned down again and looked into the car.

"He wants us to wait for him."

She straightened up again, smiling at him as he came

hurrying up, looking like a sub-tropical Ichabod Crane. When she looked down at Andrea Huse-Lorne, she was a little taken aback at her obvious irritation at both of them. Apparently it was Mrs. rather than Major Huse-Lorne who didn't like to be interrupted doing anything or going anywhere. She'd moved over and was leaning across the seat to look out.

"He looks frightfully silly, doesn't he?"

He did, really, but Betsy was a little shocked nevertheless. He looked silly to her because she wasn't used to the kind of shorts he wore, but no sillier than the other English she'd seen on the street, including a naval officer apparently fully dressed in a uniform that came to an abrupt end at his knee joints. But Andrea was used to it, and she had not smiled when she said it. Her voice seemed in fact to have a tinge of more than faint contempt.

Major Huse-Lorne had slowed down to get his breath, but he was still panting when he got to them.

"Oh, I say——"

His wife cut him off curtly. "Look, darling. If you don't mind, Betsy and I are taking a run out to have a look at Fort Charlotte. We're in a rush, rather. I've got to get back to change for lunch."

"Oh, splendid," Ramsay Huse-Lorne said. "I'll just go along, if I may."

"Oh, darling, don't be dull. Betsy and I haven't had——"

"I think it would be fun." Betsy said it before she stopped to think that after all it was Mrs. Huse-Lorne's husband and Mrs. Huse-Lorne's car. She smiled radiantly at him as she opened the back door of the car. She slipped in and pulled the door shut. "After all," she said, "it's my fault he isn't home working on his compost pile. I'm afraid I interrupted him, but he was very nice about it."

She though instantly: *that was a mistake*. Andrea Huse-Lorne's silence seemed protracted. Her shoulders seemed to stiffen slowly.

"Really?" she asked. "That's . . . interesting, Ramsay."

"Yes, Andrea." He got himself into the seat beside her. His face was not so red now. In fact it looked almost pale. As he sat stiffly erect the color seemed to come and go along the back of his sunburned neck. "It was, rather."

It was odd, but it sounded as if they were saying something to each other that was unintelligible to her but that they understood clearly. The smile on her face vanished. It was something Andrea Huse-Lorne did not like. Her mouth

140

hardened as she ripped off the brake and jerked the car out into the traffic. Betsy settled back. It had been a mistake, to bring up the compost heap, and to insist on Huse-Lorne's coming along. It was more than evident in the rigid line of Andrea's gleaming yellow head and in the way she drove, attacking every loophole in the disorderly welter of cars, taxis, carts and carriages and dodging pedestrians by close misses, as if each one of them was a personal outrage. The car seemed to be transformed into a blue demon of the same mind. It was not until they had turned off Bay Street around the hotel and back onto the West Road, along the silken, sandy shore, that Betsy let go the handle of the car and settled back without anxiety.

They came to the open fields sloping up to the ancient gray stone fortress lying along the low ridge.

"This is Fort Charlotte, Betsy," Andrea said without slowing down.

"I thought we were going to stop and show it to her."

"No. A stupid pile of old rock. It was the Country Club I wanted to show her."

On their right the turquoise sea broke in gentle white plumes along the shallow indentations of the shore, by walled gardens with bright pink and yellow and white houses behind them, the ocean stretching out beyond until sea and sky merged into hazy blue. Sea grapes, wind-torn and rugged, grew along the shore. The almonds with their falling leaves, coarse autumnal palettes of green and red and gold, the royal poincianas, their dried pods grating in the light breeze, were dull splotches of winter death in the glittering sun of eternal summer. Betsy caught her breath, her eyes sparkling. They rounded a low rocky ledge into a curving avenue of casuarina pines. Their long, slender trunks were rose-mauve and deep purple-blue in the sunlight that transformed their waving feathery branches into shifting planes of sage-green fog, as light and airy as Spanish moss. The avenue curved around a sudden little bay, its waves breaking into white foam, embroidering its elegant girdle of cream-smooth sand.

Oh, I wish Scott were here. I wish I'd waited and come with him. She forgot Charles Cavanaugh for a moment and forgot the Huse-Lornes, still silent and unfriendly in the seat in front of her.

Andrea spoke suddenly. "I suppose you showed Betsy what you found in your dead leaves and mouldy trash." They were going into the avenue of pines around the head of the little bay. The sudden quite tangible silence came only partly from the silence of the pines. The other part—taut, unpleasant—was the silence as Andrea's voice, flat and hard, came to a stop. Betsy listened. It seemed an odd question for her to ask. Perhaps it explained something.

"I thought you said you'd finished turning the heap until it rained again."

Her voice had the same flat, hard tone.

"I was not turning it," Huse-Lorne said evenly. "I was hunting a spot to put the lapis doorstop."

The car swerved sharply. Betsy glanced back. They must have hit a wet place, or an obstruction of some kind. The road was dry and clear. Andrea's shoulders were rigid, her face pale, her eyes contracted, fixed on the road ahead. Major Huse-Lorne's eyes were on the road too.

What had he said? . . . *the lapis doorstop.* She repeated the words in her mind, puzzled. Lapis meant stone—if that was really what he'd said. Lapidary, worker in precious stones. Lapis lazuli, blue stone. Lapis doorstop, stone doorstop. Was it his accent, or her hearing? Even a completely hopeless addict would not put a stone in a compost heap. She started to smile, and stopped as she saw Andrea's face in the mirror over the windshield, and saw the smile on her bright red lips. It was an unpleasant smile, amused but not pleasantly amused. It had derision in it, contempt . . . vicious, poisonous contempt.

Betsy leaned back in the seat, wishing they'd get to the Country Club and go back. The pleasure of the silent eeriness of the pine shadows was gone, the houses on either side just the sort of town and country thing you could see at Miami Beach. She was aware then that the car was moving with a different rhythm, lightly and evenly, as if Andrea's better humor, if it could be called that, had taken some of the strain out of it as well as out of her. She was certainly in something that could be called better humor. Her shoulders were not as rigid, she'd shifted her body, one arm resting easily on the open window frame. Something had happened. The attitude of her head and shoulders, the smoother rhythm of the car, seemed to express complete satisfaction . . . with herself, with everything, even with her husband. Her voice seemed to be self-satisfied too.

"You know, darling," she was saying easily. "I've been thinking that you ought to go to England and see your cousin. It's a shame we couldn't manage last autumn when

142

you wanted to go. But we're better off now. I know you want to see him before he's too awfully ill."

They were passing a broad open plain where people were playing golf. A long pink-and-white building was on the sea side of the road.

"Aren't we turning in here?" Ramsay Huse-Lorne's quiet voice asked. "This is the Country Club, Betsy."

"I thought we'd go on a bit, darling. I'd like Betsy to see the pine barrens. And our house over the hill. The view is divine from there. And I thought I'd make over all the development out here to you, Ramsay."

She turned a little, speaking to Betsy. "There's only a two percent inheritance tax here in the Bahamas."

It seemed completely irrelevant. She turned back and went coolly on. "I think, Ramsay, we'd save a good deal even at that, if we divided our property now. It would give you more leeway in helping your cousins. I know they'd rather take help from you than from me."

Whether it was something new in the calm complacency of her voice, something else there, something in the words themselves, that scratched on a half-closed door in Betsy's mind, she did not know. She knew in one clearly illuminating instant, as the door flew open, what she was hearing. She had heard it before, many times, in Mr. Steinberg's conference room at the office, as she sat off in a corner, taking down what was said. It was a deal that was being made. A deal that was not intended to look like a deal . . . the value to be received plainly stated, no statement made about what it was to be received for. She listened, fascinated. Mrs. Huse-Lorne was making a deal with her husband. Offering him a trip to England she hadn't allowed him to make the year before, offering to divide her property with him. He would be able to help his family in England.

A quick chill seemed to run up and down her spine. She saw the gooseflesh standing out on her arms. This had something to do, in some way, with the compost heap. She knew it, intuitively. Whatever was in there that he had found, that was what they were talking about. It was also about her. The hair-thin streak of alarm darted lightning-swift into her mind. Her body tensed, her mouth as dry suddenly as the ground along the road.

I suppose you showed Betsy what you found in your dead leaves and mouldy trash. I thought you said you'd finished turning the heap until it rained again.

143

I was not turning it. I was hunting a spot to put the lapis doorstop.

I thought I was putting something there that nobody would find until the rains came. Something that it was very important to me not to have found. Something that would rot away and never be found? And Major Huse-Lorne had found it. He had found it by accident. I was looking for a spot . . . That was when she had gone off the road. And he had said lapis doorstop. It was the shock of hearing him say that that had made her lose control of the car for an instant. But . . . he had also said he was trying to find a place to put it, to hide it from sight. It was when she heard that that she'd started smiling. That was when the deal was born. The contempt, the scorn, and the satisfaction all there in her face at the same time was because she'd heard he was hiding it. He'd sold out. He was open to a deal. His trying to hide . . . something that had the same significance to each of them, was all she needed.

The deal was a big one. It was important. Betsy stole a glance at Huse-Lorne. The back of his hairy, red neck was the way it had been when he first got into the car. Red, then white. The color going and coming, in waves, between the collar of his white shirt and the straggling uneven line of his straw-blond hair. *Lapis, stone.* The hair-thin streak of alarm that had shot through her had broken up into tiny, phosphorescent particles, each one alive and searing hot. *I'm in on this. I'm here somewhere. That's why we're going on. That's why we didn't stop at the Country Club.* That was why both of them ignored her, neither had pointed out anybody's house or even told her the name of the lovely little emerald-green bay dancing along the curving avenue of casuarina pines. *Lapis, rock.* Why try to hide a . . .

She knew suddenly, with a clear and distinct knowledge, what the rock was. She could hear Colonel Renfrew's voice on the porch that morning, as plainly as if he were sitting there beside her in the car. The blow on the skull, of course. We have no way of telling whether he got that when he struck the rock on the bottom of the cistern, or got it before he went in. She moved a little to let out the breath constricted in her lungs. The creeping silent steps going along with Henry's down the stone stairs. The thub, splash. A lapis doorstop, wrapped in a piece of cloth, a scarf, a kerchief. Henry's frantic unintelligible whisper. Charles Cavanaugh

144

drawing the diagram of the Huse-Lorne garden. She choked a little as she tried to swallow without making any noise that would make either of them look back and see her. If only a millionth of the shock and horror she felt seeped through into her face and eyes, they'd know she knew. And Huse-Lorne coming back from the lower terrace, striding up to the house to call the police, before he went up to her room and the police came, and the white light flooded the garden, turning her room into a barred prison cell. He must not have known it then . . . or did he? If he tried to hide the lapis doorstop, he'd know before he turned over the compost heap. When she'd interrupted him . . .

She stole another glance at the back of his head and caught her breath so sharply she thought they must have heard her. But Andrea was heaping new and greater largesse into the glittering deal, gilding the already gold-and-sterling plated lily, as the price of his silence and his support. Support of her, betrayal of Betsy Dayton and of himself. Sitting there, trying intensely to make no sound, Betsy saw what the deal was. Ramsay Huse-Lorne had bent his head down. The back of his neck was almost white now, the color all drained from it.

"And I'm terribly tired of business, darling. If you'd really take over . . . As Sir Ramsay you'd have a lot of prestige, dealing with these Bahamians, that a woman can never hope to have."

What a livid fool he must think I am, Betsy thought. *Telling him all that. Apologizing for his wife when he'd already found out she'd . . .*

Then, crawling gradually, like a wounded lizard, over the floor of her mind, it came, dragging out, slowly, stupidly, just as the other had come, first on one level too stunning for her to see the stairway leading to the second where a grimmer, more terrible fact was lying in wait for her. It was then her mouth went really dry. Her feet together on the floor pressed closer to keep them steady, her hands folded in her lap closed tighter to keep them from trembling. She shifted her body out of line in the mirror over the windshield. It was not Andrea Huse-Lorne's face she wanted to look at.

Andrea Huse-Lorne. Harriet Grantson.

She huddled closer inside herself and raised her eyes slowly to the back of Andrea Huse-Lorne's head. She was a child there again, a ten-year-old child in the back of a taxicab. The bull neck and the great hunched shoulders of the man were no longer there. The drooping pathetic shoulders of Ramsay Huse-Lorne were there, on the wrong side. And Harriet . . . Andrea or Harriet. Her hair was no longer dark and fastened in an old-fashioned bun on the back of her neck. It was glittering, shining gold, smartly turned under in a pageboy bob. Color was unimportant, it could be changed. The line of her smart shoulders could have changed too. A drooping, pleading woman looks old, an erect confident woman looks younger and totally different. And Harriet had never been the important one of the two in the front seat.

The car was going faster. The alarm in her mind sharpened. Until then overbalanced by the slow process of awakening and understanding, it was acute now, no longer to be pushed back. *This was the danger.* This was the danger that had been stalking her silently and treacherously, that she'd walked into without knowing it, blinded every step of the way, as her father had been blinded and betrayed. And killed . . . It was not Charles Cavanaugh. He'd been trying to protect her. It was this woman. Andrea Huse-Lorne. Poisoner and thief. Without thinking, she moved her hand toward the door of the car and looked out. She stared with sickening horror at the road she'd forgotten to look at.

They had passed the last house. She hadn't noticed how fast or how far they'd gone. There was nothing. Nothing. Not even a native hut. She saw one then and started again to reach for the door. But it was empty, deserted. The coconut thatch hung down rotten and gaping above the shack not as big as a backyard chicken house. No windows or doors, no children. Nothing to tell there was still a human being within a thousand miles. The pine barrens . . . Tall, weedy trees growing out of the rock, the bush, a rank unlovely growth, clutching its thirsty hold into the eroded shallows of the stony substratum, creeping evil stuff as dry and barren as the rock and the pines. Off to the right of the uneven road was the sea. Even the sea had changed. The smiling blue waves breaking gently on the velvet sand had changed as fantastically as the earth the instant it was no longer watered and coaxed and goaded into cultivation. The sheltered beaches and the soft, lovely sand were gone. There was nothing but the rock, the rollers smashing against it and over it . . . black rock growing out of the pools of foam as the waves thrashed by it, to gather and burst again against the massive low-lying coast. As barren as the pines, as unfriendly and dangerous as the bush and thorn and tangled vines along the road. This was the wilderness. The word had never had any meaning to Betsy before.

"I wouldn't try to jump for it if I were you, dear." The car speeded up again. "After all, this is what you came down here for, isn't it? You thought my husband would help you—that's why you waited for him in Bay Street. You're frightfully naive still, my child. He's as sick of being poor as I was. He's not as big a fool as you thought, Elizabeth. He's perfectly aware that if you . . . *unmask* me—as I suppose you think of it . . . he won't have to worry about two per cent income tax. Poverty isn't very pleasant, not when it's so simple to avoid."

Poverty. As if she and her mother hadn't known as much about poverty as Ramsay Huse-Lorne had ever known. And all because of this woman. Harriet Grantson had left them with a horrible debt they'd had to pay. And her mother had believed her father was a thief and a suicide. And Harriet Grantson had made it appear that he was running off, with his secretary, adding a personal shame, belittling all the relationship between them. She heard Andrea saying the name "Elizabeth" as she'd heard her say it before Scott had called her "Betsy," the afternoon before. It scratched at something in her mind, but she let it go. What she'd just said was more important. This is what you came down here for, isn't it? Harriet Grantson as well as Henry, and Charles Cavanaugh, had thought she knew, had thought that was why she'd come. *And if they hadn't thought it, I never would have known.* All her life she'd have been in ignorance, never fully living down the disgrace and the unhappiness that clung in her mind to her father's memory. She brought her hand back from the door handle. In a sense, there was a kind of compensation, knowing the truth, even if she did have to pay this way for it.

"And believe me when I say there's no use trying to jump for it," Andrea said coolly. "I've got a gun this time, dear. Uncle Charles kindly left it for me in the pavilion on Hog Island." The ironic lilt in her voice underlined cold deadly confidence. "I had to go over this morning because Henry Grantson's box was there, not in the cabin of the boat. Ramsay's friend Renfrew overlooked that—probably because the keys were in his pocket and I already had them.—I'd hate to have to shoot you. I've never liked guns. Out here no one will ever hear the sound."

Betsy heard her own voice then. It sounded strangely far away, but it was steady.

"Did you know that Charles Cavanaugh was a taxi driver in Hoboken, in 1939?"

The car lurched, swerved off the road and back. "What did you say? Say that again . . ." Mrs. Huse-Lorne's voice was harsh and vicious.

Ahead of them the road branched . . . for the first time, Betsy thought. She picked up the white glove lying in her lap and slipped it out of the window as they entered the right fork. She did not hope too poignantly that it would be there if Scott came. It was all the hope there was. And she was thankful she was not in any of the panic she had been in before, either a moment ago when she'd first seen the pine barrens and knew what wilderness meant, or before, last night. The panic was gone. Her life might be lost anyway, but she knew it was lost if she lost her head now. This was reality.

If I just hadn't left that stupid note. They'll sit around and wait. Wait lunch until it's cold . . .

"Aren't you going to the house, Andrea?" Huse-Lorne asked quietly.

"I'm stopping here." Her voice was flat and deadly. "I didn't recognize Charles Cavanaugh. I see this all now. It wasn't Henry I wanted after all."

"Scott took the cyanide you put in my aspirin to the Hospital this morning," Betsy said. "You must have had it left over from what you killed my father with. You can't go on forever killing people and getting away with it."

It seemed to her that all she could hope to do was make her angry now, upset her some way, shake her frightening self-confidence, as she'd shaken it asking if she'd known about Charles Cavanaugh. She slid the other glove cautiously out. If only Scott . . . But she couldn't think of him. It did wrenching painful things to her insides, just saying his name to herself in her mind. She looked away from the blond pageboy hair and at Ramsay Huse-Lorne. He had turned a little in the seat. His lips were almost waxen under the drooping straw of his mustache. He turned a little farther, just enough to shoot her a sudden glance. It was lightning brief, but her heart rose with a sudden, bursting glow. He'd

148

not sold out. He was on her side still. She felt her knees shaking together, her heart leap into her throat.

"I wouldn't try any tricks, Ramsay," Andrea Huse-Lorne said. "You haven't fooled me. I've trusted men who pray. I'm stopping now. Get out, both of you."

21

At the bottom of the hill, with Bay Street in front of him, Scott Beckwith came to an abrupt standstill, looking right and left and across the road, sweeping his eyes along for Betsy's bright, lithe figure. Take away the gaudy sunlight, he thought, and the carriages with their stained pink-red curtains and tinkling bells, and all the sub-tropical glamour and colonial West Indian flavor, and it was Main Street in some sleepy southern market town on Saturday morning, people moving in a desultory, leisurely way, not hurrying or crowding, stopping to look and maybe to buy. He forced himself to stand still and look up and down, and across to the other side again. If she was in a shop she'd wander out in a minute, he'd see her then. But he did not see her. Minutes could be scarce. He forced himself to stop his pumping heart and fevered mind as well as his feet. There were only five short blocks where she'd be likely to shop, if she was shopping as she'd said she was going to do. There weren't many places in Naussau that a newcomer was likely to wander off to. All he had to do was wait right there.

He stirred uneasily. If she wasn't there . . . If it weren't Betsy, he thought quickly, but just any girl he knew, who was walking in instant and hideous danger, and it was up to him to get hold of her, and he knew whom the danger came from, what would he do? He took one more sweeping glance up and down the street, turned and dashed into the hotel there on the corner. He should have stopped first at the Huse-Lornes'. The telephone was the next best thing.

"Mahdam has not come in." The soft, Bahamian lilt at the other end seemed to rebuke his own strident impatience. "Sir Ramsay has gone out too, sir." He pressed down the bar, made a new connection and held it a moment. "Sir Ramsay." This was courtesy stuff with a vengeance. He lifted his finger and dialled Government House. She'd said she was going there, to the Gymkhana Committee meeting.

"Sorry." The brisk English voice promptly dismissed that. "The meeting is tomorrow. Mrs. Huse-Lorne must have made a mistake."

What next? He remembered the pavilion. Maybe, on an off-chance, if Betsy thought she was in anybody's hair . . . He strode back into the street and hurried along, glancing around occasionally and into the shops as he passed. He tore into the Square. None of the boatmen had taken her across to the Island. Then as he started out of the Square he groaned aloud. Mr. Fallon, the old gentleman with the white hair that looked like a wig above his sun-blackened mummy's face, was getting out of a taxi to take the Club boat back to the Island. He had his golf clubs over his shoulder and his straw market basket in his hand. If he should buttonhole him . . .

"Hello there, Scott." Mr. Fallon put a hand out to stop him.

"Good morning, sir."

He would have barged away, except for the grace of God and an old man who liked a pretty girl.

"Looking for that very good-looking young lady of yours?" Mr. Fallon asked waggishly.

Scott stopped short. "Have you seen her?"

The mummy face smiled happily. "Out by the golf course." Scott's heart was a leaden plummet in his stomach. He forced himself to stand and wait. "With the Huse-Lornes. In that blue car of hers."

He'd known horribly what was coming before it came. But if Huse-Lorne was there . . .

"Nice fellow, Ramsay. Don't care much for Madam, personally."

"You wouldn't know where they were——"

"No idea. Past the Club, on out, you know."

Mr. Fallon had his arm in a firm grip. "It's none of my business, Scott, but Cavanaugh hasn't been taken in by that woman, has he? We've always managed to keep her out. Be a pity if he lets her get a toehold, using his pavilion. Anderson said she was over there this morning, inside and out, looking as if she owned it. Perhaps you could drop a word . . . awkward for the rest of——"

"Right, sir. Thanks for telling me."

He didn't stop to help the old gentleman on the boat, as he normally would have done. Andrea Huse-Lorne had Betsy off in the wilderness somewhere. She'd been at the pavilion.

151

She must have had the keys. Henry's keys, he thought quickly. That wasn't the point. Charles had guns over there. Two of them, upstairs in the bedroom cabinet, with shells to go with them. Charles was a gun man, always had them around, even down here and in spite of his sister's objections. If Andrea wanted one . . .

He turned and went quickly across the Square. What to do now? He had no car. He didn't know where the Huse-Lornes were likely to go. He was a little sick, suddenly. His eyes fell then on the bright, yellow buildings in the public square. The police. The guy from the C.I.D. This was their time to function.

He ran up the rattletrap wooden steps and up and down through the ramshackle labyrinth that led to the office of the head of the Criminal Investigation Division of the Bahamian Police. The officer who had come with Colonel Renfrew that morning was sitting at his desk. Lawson. Captain Lawson. Scott's heart sank. British. He'd never get any action here. They were too nice, too politely detached, to snap out of the colonial lassitude and move. And the Huse-Lornes *belonged*. He was just an American.

"Look here," he said. "I haven't got time to explain. You've got to take my word for it. Andrea Huse-Lorne has got my girl out the West Road. Mrs. Huse-Lorne killed Henry Grantson. She's going to kill Miss Dayton if we don't get out there and stop her."

Captain Lawson took one long, searching look at him, pushed back his papers, was on his feet and had his cap before Scott had more than finished what he was saying.

They went quickly out. "Huse-Lorne is with them," Scott went on.

It seemed to stop the C.I.D. man a little. "If Sir Ramsay is with them——"

"Sir Ramsay . . . ?"

"It came through in a press despatch this morning. They've been trying to get him on the phone. The baronet died, he inherits. I expect the title's all that's left."

They went down the wooden steps to the garage behind the open shed. Two subordinates detached themselves from nowhere, it seemed to Scott. The car moved through the streets.

"Where would they go?" he asked. "Where would they take her? They passed the golf course going toward South Bay not too long ago."

"The Huse-Lornes have a house out there," Captain Lawson said. "We'll try that. You'd better explain a little, Beckwith. I wasn't entirely satisfied with Lady Huse-Lorne's account of things this morning. Her attitude was a little . . . casual. A bit callous, even." He smiled faintly. "As a matter of fact, I was just looking over her dossier. Your consul sent it on."

"The American consul? What——"

"Passport information. As an American citizen, of course, she didn't need a passport to come here. She went to England with Sir Ramsay in 1946. Your consul arranged her passport from Washington. She hadn't got a birth certificate or her other marriage papers. They got affidavits from the town she was born in. Alabama. Her maiden name was Andrea Palmer. The clerk at the court house there happened to have gone to school with her."

Scott looked at him blankly. "But . . . that isn't possible. Her name is Harriet Grantson. The little man who was killed last night was her father."

Captain Lawson shrugged. "Passports have been obtained on fraudulent information," he remarked dryly. "Even in your country. I have no evidence it was true in Lady Huse-Lorne's case. You'd better explain. I can't, you know, just walk in and arrest Lady Huse-Lorne without some substantial evidence. She's a respected person in Nassau."

They rounded the low stone ledge on the shore by Emerald Beach, and headed into the avenue of casuarina pines around the head of the shallow, sunlit bay. It was silent and somber as they drove into the whispering shadows.

"It won't be far now. If we're both right. They may be lunching pleasantly at the Country Club, of course."

Scott pulled himself back from the abyss where fear and the intolerable snail's pace of the hurtling police car had led him. There was no use thinking about anything until he found her.

"I don't know what you'd call substantial evidence," he said quietly and dispassionately. He had Henry Grantson's note with him. He handed it to Lawson, and told him what he knew. It was unbelievably neat and cunning, as he went over it again, filling the gaps with what Charles had said. "Harriet Grantson would damned well have to kill him—her own father. Lady Huse-Lorne wouldn't want him hanging around. And Miss Dayton's the only other person left, beside my uncle, who could possibly recognize her. I gather that's

153

why Cavanaugh came down when she did . . . hoping she'd recognize her too."

Andrea Huse-Lorne held the automatic in her scarlet-nailed hand. It glinted blue-black in the sunlight. She motioned toward the gray rock that made a solid wall at the land side of the road. Her voice raised above the sullen roar and crash of the waves was as vicious and deadly as the gun. "Get over there, Ramsay. Stand by Elizabeth. And don't try to be noble."

Andrea backed like a cat around the front of the car. It was a barrier between them, protecting her. Her hand with the gun rested on the chromium-plated figure on the hood. Betsy stood there. It was extraordinary how little feeling she had, as long as she didn't think of Scott or her mother at home. She put them quickly out of her mind, lifted her chin, looking at Andrea, brown eyes meeting blue across the narrow road. Actually and to her surprise, all she felt was contempt, withering scorn, for the woman there. Andrea was the one raddled with fear. That was what had driven her, it was what still held her hand now. She couldn't just shoot both of them and be done with it. The smile on Betsy's lips struck home. She saw the spasm of fury that curdled the flesh of Andrea's face, saw her eyes contract until they were livid slits between her lashes. Her hand tightened on the gun.

Betsy heard her voice again, still far off, still steady.

"You're afraid to shoot. You can poison people, and lock them in buildings you've set on fire. Hit them over the head with a doorstop in the dark. You're afraid to pull the trigger of a gun in broad daylight. Because you're a bully and a coward. You know you can't go back and lie any more, and be believed. Because Charles Cavanaugh is still there. The taxi driver from Hoboken. He knows who you are."

The blue eyes sharpened with a bright glitter. Mrs. Huse-Lorne's hand tensed on the weapon in her hand. Her tongue flicked out at the corner of her mouth. Her stare fixed on Betsy was mocking.

"No, Elizabeth. I somehow don't think he does."

Betsy heard her name again, the way her father used to say it and as Andrea Huse-Lorne had said it twice, and now a third time. The key faintly turning, before, in the rusty lock of some long-shut door in her memory, turned sharply now, caught and released the closed door, flinging it open. The fantastic illumination concealed behind it shot out. She caught her breath. She knew now. She knew why Andrea Huse-Lorne had not recognized Charles Cavanaugh.

"Oh, I . . . I'm afraid he does, Andrea."

Betsy moved her eyes for an instant to Major Huse-Lorne and saw that his stuttering, feeble confirmation masked a purpose. The angle between his feet and hers had changed. He was moving forward almost imperceptibly. She looked back quickly, meeting the blue animal eyes that had started shifting, and spoke sharply.

"He does know you."

The eyes slashed back.

"He said so, last night. I heard him. You heard him. Henry Grantson had a daughter."

The smile deepened on the red lips. Huse-Lorne was closer.

"So Charles Cavanaugh knows Henry Grantson's daughter didn't die some years ago. He knows I'm Harriet Grantson . . ."

"*No,*" Betsy Dayton said. "*She did die. She died in the burning warehouse. Ethel Gurney didn't. You're Ethel Gurney. He knows it and I know it.—You're poor Ethel Gurney!*"

Her voice, stinging with contempt, swept across the narrow wind-torn road carved out of the rock, lashing at the woman there as the wind lashed the sea-grapes clinging to the sand. Andrea Huse-Lorne opened her mouth, trying to speak, her body shaking.

"I know you now. You learned to say my name that way from my father. He's the only other person who ever called me that. Harriet called me Lizabeth. That's why you didn't recognize Charles Cavanaugh. You never knew him. You never saw him except at a distance. Oh, I know you now. Poor Ethel Gurney! Your mean blue eyes . . . Harriet's eyes were brown and soft, cow's eyes, not devil's. And I should have seen it. You received the money from the bank that afternoon. You knew everything in the chemists' stockroom. And you could do anything with Harriet, she was always coming back to do your work when you had a headache. She hated you but she was afraid of you. So was I. The only time we ever had any fun was when you were in the hospital——"

She broke off, the light in her blazing eyes brightening

155

with a sudden flash of instantaneous remembrance. "You had an operation in the hospital, Ethel Gurney . . . You've got a——"

Ethel Gurney took one jerking backward step, raising her hand to her head. Huse-Lorne leaped. She caught herself, white-faced, before her hand had got to her bleached golden hair, whipped her hand down and fired. The sound cracked and crashed against the solid face of the rock wall. Huse-Lorne's white shirt spurted blood. He caught her hand, grappling with her, swinging himself between her and Betsy. Behind her, standing there half-paralyzed, Betsy heard the continued urgent blast of the car horn. Huse-Lorne staggered, trying to hold her with one arm, and Ethel Gurney pulled away. She stood there swaying, took one look at the car, raised the gun to her head and fired a second shot. The gun fell with a crash on the hood of the car and slipped down, ringing along the fender, to the pavement. Huse-Lorne, slumping to the ground, pulled himself up, and crawling over, knelt there beside her body.

Betsy ran toward the road. "Scott! Scott!" She knew no sound he could hear was coming from her lips. The car pulled up with a scream of brakes. She saw a white shining patch in the hand that was already opening the door. It was her glove. It was Scott. She sank down in the road. "It isn't Harriet. It's Ethel Gurney." She was trying to tell him, but it was a faint whisper on her lips as everything closed in and she slipped away into unconsciousness there on the wilderness road.

22

"Quit saying it was stupid of you, Betsy dear." Scott drew her closely to him and kissed her tenderly. "You're wonderful. Gosh, I don't know what I'd have done . . . I love you, Betsy." He lapsed into happy inarticulateness. She was like that poor devil Ramsay, in the hospital with his shoulder practically blasted off, keeping on saying if he'd done it properly he could have kept her from raising the gun to her own head when she saw it was no use. You'd think he'd rather have it like this. This way the police could do something to smooth it over.

He kissed her again, and looked up to the veranda. His father was there. Captain Lawson had been there and seen Charles Cavanaugh. It was all over, like a nightmare when the sun streams through the blinds and the day has come. He and Betsy moved slowly across the crab grass to where John Beckwith was sitting, the paper on his knees. He picked it up.

"It's rather malicious, I suppose," he said, "but I can't help thinking it's a sort of pity Andrea can't read the final account of Lady Huse-Lorne's worth and value to the community. It's all recorded here."

"Ramsay seems to feel she was spared a kind of ultimate disappointment," Scott said. "It's a nice way to look at it. But he's a nice guy."

"He is," John Beckwith said. He looked at them. "I was sorry I couldn't get hold of you to tell you she wasn't Harriet Grantson. I made it out myself, slowly, with all Charles's 'she's and 'her's.' "

He gazed off over the garden a moment.

"You know, I have an idea Charles will be all right now? He talked again this morning to Lawson and me. He had a . . . a kind of double guilt. It's a painful story, because Charles isn't as ruthless or as callous as he'd like to believe. He was sick of Harriet. He'd push her off, but she'd ooze back like a jellyfish—one of those soft persistent people always ready to forgive. And when he didn't meet her, she'd go around the waterfront hunting for him. He couldn't risk much of that, with the job he was doing, and he was really stuck with her. He'd taken her to the office that night to do Gurney's work—she'd told him Gurney had a headache. What makes him a first-class swine, then, is that he thought of the fire as an act of God to get Harriet off his neck. He thought it was an accident, at first, just as he thought Dayton had had a heart attack.

"He didn't go to the police, at first, because he expected Gurney to come forward. When she didn't, he salved his conscience, if any, by arguing that if he got mixed up with the police at all, he wouldn't be of any more use to Naval Intelligence, and he was on a hot lead. But he was inquiring around at the same time. When he heard it was cyanide and not a heart that killed Jerome Dayton, he began putting things together. By that time it had been written off as accident and suicide, and he let it go again. He found that if he slugged himself out every night, he could sleep without having nightmares. Then he found out that Henry Grantson had been hunting for Harriet, and had figured things out as he had. He took Henry on, trying to fool himself a third time: they'd find Ethel Gurney and hand her over to the police. All the time he was drinking heavily to keep from having to face himself and what he'd really done."

John Beckwith shook his head, remembering the change that had come over Charles Cavanaugh.

"When the war came then, I used to think he was deliberately trying to get himself knocked off, and of course he was. Instead, all he got was medals. And when it was over, he started drinking again. And I think he's through, now. He wasn't a heel, and he couldn't stand seeing himself act like one."

He knocked his pipe out and put it in his pocket. "As a matter of fact, he and Henry did a first-class job of investigation. They traced her through passport information. Andrea Palmer was a girl from Alabama, all right, and the clerk in the court house did know her. She'd been to school with him. But so had Ethel Gurney. Andrea Palmer went to New York and died, in poverty and unknown. Gurney was perfectly safe in taking her name and bleaching her hair to match the real Andrea's. They found her name in the same classroom records, and they went on from there. Charles

158

knew about the scar on her neck. They really weren't absolutely sure about Mrs. Huse-Lorne—that was more than just deliberately trying to deceive himself. Charles hoped, of course, that you might remember. I'm truly thankful for one thing, that Henry kept him from killing her himself."

The sultry fire was smouldering still in Betsy's brown eyes.

"The one thing I can't forgive her," she said slowly, "is making the plane reservations and putting her clothes there with my father's. Doing it herself, pretending he was in love with her and running away with her. That, and leaving Harriet Grantson something in her will. It . . . it was a foul, offensive thing. I might be able to pity her, not hate her, if she hadn't done that."

"Don't, Betsy," Scott said gently. "Try to forget it, sweetie."

She smiled at him. "I suppose I ought to have recognized her. But . . . Ethel Gurney was such a . . . a frusty, rat's-nesty sort of person. I didn't know all she needed was a scrub brush and a bottle of peroxide and some smart clothes to make her into Andrea. And she seemed so horribly old to me, when I was ten."

John Beckwith smiled a little. "At least you know now, about all of it, Betsy," he said gravely. He added, "Charles wants to see you. Don't expect him to talk about it. He probably won't talk at all, but he asked to see you. You don't mind going up for a moment, do you?"

She shook her head.

"I'd like to see him. I . . . I've got a letter that belongs to him. I'd like to give it to him. It's a copy of a letter to him. It was in the Huse-Lorne mail this morning. I . . . I had it sent there when I . . . I didn't know. I haven't opened it, and it's his, not mine."

She hesitated a moment. "There's one thing that I'd like, very much. If Scott doesn't mind. I'd like it if . . . if the money she stole, that Ramsay wants to give back . . . if we don't take it. I'd like him to do all the things she promised him out there—when she was trying to make the deal, make him sell out and be on her side, not mine."

John Beckwith smiled again, looking at her for a moment without saying anything.

"I think Scott will agree to that, Betsy. And I think we can make Huse-Lorne see what you mean." A dry light gleamed in his gray eyes. "A poor wife is much easier to get along with than a rich one."

159

"So I've heard," Scott said with a sudden grin. "It's okay with me, Betsy."

"So go along and see Charles, will you, Betsy?" John Beckwith said. "Scott can spare you that long."

"That long and no longer." Scott smiled at her. "And don't call him Mr. Cavanaugh. Call him Uncle Charles, Betsy."

She shook her head, the sudden laughter sparkling in her eyes.

"I'll just call him Charles," she said. "And some day I'll tell him it was because I fell in love with him when I was ten that I fell in love with you when I was twenty-two."

She stopped in front of him as she went toward the stairs.

"So maybe you'll kiss me just once before I go."

Her face clouded. "Oh, dear!" she said. "That's what poor little Harriet always used to say to him . . ."

Scott smiled down into her upturned face. "But I like it. On the other hand, Charles certainly knows how to manage the dames . . . and he makes 'em wait. So run along, little dame, run along . . . and hurry back."

CPSIA information can be obtained
at www.ICGtesting.com
Printed in the USA
BVOW09s0938050418
512455BV00001B/9/P